A TUNISIAN TALE

A TUNISIAN TALE

Hassouna Mosbahi

Translated by
Max Weiss

The American University in Cairo Press
Cairo   New York

First published in 2011 by
The American University in Cairo Press
113 Sharia Kasr el Aini, Cairo, Egypt
420 Fifth Avenue, New York, NY 10018
www.aucpress.com

Dar el Kutub No. 24412/11
ISBN 978 977 416 480 4

Dar el Kutub Cataloging-in-Publication Data

Mosbahi, Hassouna
        A Tunisian Tale/ Hassouna Mosbahi.—Cairo: The American University in Cairo Press, 2011
        p.   cm.
        ISBN 978 977 416 480 4
        1. Arabic fiction
        I. Title
        892.73

1 2 3 4 5 6 7 8   14 13 12 11

Designed by Fatiha Bouzidi
Printed in Egypt

"There is no folly of the beasts of the earth which is not infinitely outdone by the madness of men."

Herman Melville, *Moby Dick*

THE SON

Now my soul has calmed, and its volcanoes have quieted down. Those conflagrations that for many years used to eat away at my body have been extinguished and nothing remains of them but clumps of ash. Here I am now, as cold as the dead. This cell is as narrow as a tomb, and just as cold. Everything on the inside and on the outside suggests I've already crossed over that bridge to the other world, the unknown world that everyone fears even though we all know we're going to wind up there sooner or later. Before they ever threw me in jail and slammed the thick iron door shut behind me, I had seen myself dead, even as my heart still pounded and my senses were as heightened as those of a cat burglar. I can safely say that the frowning men who will be entrusted with my execution at dawn, those whose cold stares have been with them since they first fell out of their mother's bellies, won't get the satisfaction they've become accustomed to receiving upon executing their duty, because all they're going to find in this cold narrow cell is a cold corpse, nothing more and nothing less. In that moment they'll be as deflated as those who go out hunting and come back empty-handed, but that won't prevent them from carrying out the dirty work they willingly signed up for. Maybe they think that hanging miserable creatures like me assures a place for them in heaven. As for me, I'm interested in neither heaven nor hell.

Since I will have already departed this life some time before, my heart won't beat with panic upon hearing their heavy footsteps on the cement corridor at dawn, and I won't shiver as those silent, mute, and frowning men lead me to the gallows. I won't shed a single tear for the world I leave behind at twenty-four years of age. I won't beg them for mercy or compassion. No, my lips will be sealed, my eyes vacant, and my body as stiff as a board, no longer concerned with things like how to skin the ewe after its slaughter.

THE MOTHER

I speak from beyond the grave. Can you believe this, O living people? Your response doesn't matter much to me because I can't hear it anyway, but let me assure you that just a short while ago the merciful angel whispered to inform me that I can address you from the furthest reaches of eternal darkness. What a treat for you, and for me, too! I had always believed that speaking to you would become impossible once I departed your world and turned into a clump of ash. So listen up, and I'll tell you my story from start to finish. I'll regale you with all of its details. They may please you at times, horrify you at others, and might even make you feel sympathy for me and take pity upon me, or else become repulsed and then recoil in disgust. Anything's possible. But rest assured that I'll always be honest with you, and I won't neglect to mention a single detail, no matter how pretty or ugly it may seem, because I know all too well that you are just as curious as the people of M Slum, where I lived ever since leaving my faraway village at the age of nineteen, up until that simmering summer day when flames consumed my body. In the real world, the people of M Slum—from the toddler who has just managed to take his first steps, all the way up to the old man kneeling at the doorstep of his goddamned house waiting for Azrael to take him away—used to spy on me night and day, through the keyholes of their doors, from their windows, rooftops, and balconies. They used to keep tabs on me. They would dispatch unemployed and broke young men—and there were a lot of them in the neighborhood—to gather information about me, to find out who was going in and out of my

3

house. Most of the men were also out of work, and they'd spend hours on end in those filthy cafés, smoking and playing cards, gossiping about me even more than they ever talked about soccer matches or about Palestine, Iraq, and Afghanistan. They'd embellish upon what were primarily invented and fraudulent stories they'd heard before with still other stories that were ripped from the fabric of their imagination, which would become more and more fanciful whenever the matter concerned me in particular. Women would do the very same thing, spraying gasoline on the fire until their sharp tongues had transformed me into a terrible ogress who not only spread evil and vice and corruption throughout M Slum but throughout the capital as well, all around the country even. Most of the inhabitants were migrants from the mountains and the distant deserts who had fled famines and plagues. In spring and summer M Slum teems with gnats and all kinds of stinging insects like scorpions; in the fall it buzzes with relentless flies; and in winter it gets covered with mud and clay. The youths and men and women in that miserable slum would get creative in setting up traps to make me fall down, but I'd manage to find a way out somehow, in what always seemed like a miracle.

None of this should be too strange or surprising. Those people had suckled on wickedness and vileness and depravity along with their mother's milk, and their spirits would only be at peace once they had succeeded in causing so-and-so to fall into one of their repeatedly set traps, once they had successfully sowed evil here or there. The men constantly insulted me, seeking revenge because I had always despised them, loathed their filthiness, and recoiled from their vile ugliness. Whenever they tried to lure me in or get close to me I would stop them with violence and severity. Many of them would treat me kindly in secret, though, sending me romantic love letters; some would confess to me whenever I walked by how their hearts would nearly stop beating when I was around. But as soon as they got home or sat down in one of those miserable little cafés where they were always hanging out, they'd start flaying me, tearing at my flesh, and they wouldn't quit until their tongues wore out and turned to stone inside their putrid mouths. As for the women, they intentionally tried to hurt me and tarnish my reputation out of sheer jealousy, making up stories about how bad I smelled because not a single one of them could compete with my beautiful body, my splendid appearance, my honeyed voice, my wide pitch-black eyes or my irresistible femininity, all of which was confirmed to me by everyone who had ever loved me or cared about me.

4

But I'd better just forget all about them, if only for a little while, and get back to telling you about my life, which is more important, in all its sweetness and bitterness, ups and downs, joy and tears as well as its straight paths, as straight as a ruler, and others crooked and zigzagging like the paths goats follow up in the craggy mountains.

My life began in the village of A, which was surrounded by almond and olive groves, was ringed with cactus, and was famous all over the country not only for its premium olive oil and its delicious prickly pears, but also for its pickpockets. That's right, its infamous pickpockets who are scattered throughout the country, especially in the capital and the large coastal cities that attract a lot of foreign tourists. They are considered specialists in matters of petty crime within the security apparatus and many others say they have a soft touch that is unparalleled by the pickpockets from any other region. Sons inherit this skill from their fathers. I knew some of them when I was a little girl, and there were even more of them around back then because the poverty was so much worse than it is today. I remember one of them was called Ammar "the Blind." He wasn't literally blind but suffered from some sort of an eye condition. This malady worked to his advantage, though, because everyone would assume he was incapable of discerning what was hidden in their pockets or what they were holding in their hands and, therefore, they would more easily fall into his trap. Ammar the Blind used to wear a long gray shirt that reached all the way down to his ankles, no matter what season it was, and would place on his egg-shaped head a skullcap that had lost all its color from being worn so much. He wouldn't keep whatever he had done to his victims to himself, transforming it all instead into entertaining and stirring stories that could make those who listened to them laugh so hard their stomachs would ache. As for him, he never laughed; he would only go so far as to let a sly smile be drawn across his lips. One story he used to tell has remained in my memory until this very moment, about how he once trailed after a dim-witted peasant of the Ouled Ayyar from the market in our village all the way to Siliana in order to snatch the wad of cash he had concealed in his inner coat pocket. Ammar the Blind would narrate the details in his languid voice: "It was a bitter cold winter's day, so cold that the people were shivering despite the qashabiyas and the heavy, hooded cloaks they had wrapped around themselves, when I noticed this short man with a big head and puffy cheeks stuffing a wad of cash into his inner coat pocket. The job seemed too tough for me at first because of the thick qashabiya he was wearing, but the stupidity and idiocy in his eyes encouraged me to go for it, in spite of the dangers and the difficulties. After devouring a hot fatira with two eggs on top the man hopped aboard the bus heading for Maktar, and I did the same but couldn't find a seat right next to him. When we arrived in Maktar he ducked into a crowded restaurant and ordered two kilos of grilled meat and a serving of liver, polishing it all off in short order even as my stomach growled. The extreme cold was making my already bad mood even worse and I considered just leaving the man in peace and heading back. But just then I told myself, *Have patience, Ammar the Blind, and you'll get what you deserve in the end, for God is always with those who are patient.* After licking his lips for a long time, savoring the fat that was left all over them, he paid his bill and headed back to the station and jumped on a bus bound for Siliana. This time, luck was on my side and I found a seat beside him. I was so close that my right knee grazed his left. En route I lied to him, of course, telling him I was a lamb merchant from Sidi Bouzid and that I was on my way to Siliana for the first time in my life to visit a relative who worked there as a police officer. Then I started telling him funny stories that lightened up his dreariness that seemed to be inborn. When we pulled into Siliana, the chaotic crowdedness helped me to snatch the wad of cash from the depths of his coat pocket just as we stepped off the bus, while he stared dumbfounded at all the people's faces, as if he had just clambered out of a shadowy cave. In order to avoid suspicion and any checkpoints, I returned to the village on foot, following the riverbeds and the craggiest roads. I spent half of that wad of cash on a cow for my mother—may God grant her long life—and some other things she needed; with the other half, I bought myself a better winter than I think I'll ever have for the rest of my life!" And when the people asked him, "But Ammar, how did you manage to get your hand inside the inner coat pocket of the Ayyari if he was wrapped up in a heavy qashabiya?" Ammar the Blind would calmly reply, "That's a secret trick of the trade. Then again, maybe my sweet voice had him convinced I was a guardian angel who would never bring him any harm!"

I can also remember how my mother—may God have mercy upon her—used to love the stories and adventures of Ammar the Blind. She would invite him over to our house whenever she had the chance. We spent happy times with him because he could always transform everything connected to the world of pickpocketing and thievery into delightful stories that were good for the soul. Until one time, Ammar the Blind himself walked into a trap. That was in Kairouan, in front of the Great Mosque. His mark this time was an elderly German tourist who started screaming and hollering as soon as she felt his hand slip inside her handbag. People immediately rushed to her aid. And that's how Ammar the Blind got carted off to jail with blood gushing from his mouth, as curses rained down upon him from every direction: "Shame on you! Shame on you! You've disgraced us in front of foreigners!" As the people angrily denounced him, he hung his head in shame. After he got out of jail, his hair quickly turned white, his teeth fell out one after another, his eyes became narrow slits, his gait got all confused, he lost so much weight that he appeared to be nothing but skin and bones, he quit telling his stories and tall tales, and he stopped leaving his house except when it was absolutely necessary. He remained like that until he was found dead in his bed. That was almost a year before I left the village.

THE SON

When the judge handed down his guilty verdict after long and difficult deliberations, I breathed a sigh of relief because that was just what I had been hoping for with all my heart. There was nothing left in the world that could attract me or delight my soul. I whispered to myself, "Welcome, O beautiful death!"

All eyes were fixed on me, the eyes of those who had decided my fate and those who happened to be present in the courtroom. Many people had come for one obvious reason, as my lawyer informed me, namely, that my case had riveted people all over the country. From the rich who live in fancy villas to the poor who are unable to put dinner on the table two nights in a row; from the educated women who make speeches in Parliament and who teach at universities to those who are illiterate and who stammer when reciting the Fatiha. The lawyer would bring me magazines and newspapers and I'd follow the details of my case as if it were the issue of Palestine or Iraq.

Some even chose my story as a headline for their front page. *Headline!* That was a new vocabulary word for me, but that affable lawyer with cheeks as rosy red as a young lady who is thrilled to be single was constantly repeating it. Over time I came to understand what it meant thanks to my own personal effort, without having to ask him or anyone else for help. I say "anyone else" because in prison there are always other lawyers just like him who I could ask, as well as professors, doctors, engineers, CEOs, and former political notables. Obviously they had all broken the law and committed crimes; perhaps they'd even committed murder or embezzled from the state coffers or the institutions where they worked; perhaps they'd done other embarrassing things. They wouldn't have been in prison along with me and thousands of others otherwise. Still, they all seemed nice enough, well behaved and well mannered. Perhaps even those who were always glowering, frowning, or who rarely spoke also deserved such complimentary descriptions. None of them ever scowled directly in my face or insulted me personally with an unkind word or looked at me spitefully even though I knew for certain that they were completely familiar with my case because they were all addicted to reading newspapers and magazines. Some of those noteworthy prisoners would occasionally utter pearls of wisdom, telling me, for example, how all mothers give birth to free men who therefore must live as free men. I wouldn't comment, but just nod my head in agreement lest I get mixed up in a conversation that would reveal my ignorance about matters of wisdom. There was a skinny young man who was about thirty years old, with a small head and whose bones just about poked through his skin. Whenever I went to clean his cell he would try and talk to me about injustices that took place all over the country, about this and about that. But he stopped doing that in the end, possibly because he became convinced there was no point in carrying on a conversation about such things with a young man like me, who had severed all his connections with the real world and who was no longer concerned with whatever good or evil it contained. By doing so he brought some relief to both of us. There was another man of about fifty who kept his beard carefully trimmed at all times, as if it were his own private garden that was hidden from sight, and who insisted on wearing long white robes even on the coldest days of winter. On one occasion he whispered to me, "Heaven is beneath the feet of mothers!" Of course, I knew that this was a barb directed straight at me, but I didn't respond to him in the slightest. I would have liked to tell him that what he said was beautiful and sound but that reality isn't so. In our country mothers are like cheap racks where everything gets hung. People wipe their hands all over their mother as if she were a scrap of paper in a public toilet. She's cursed and insulted all the time. A child bickering with one of his peers starts cursing the other one's mother early on. He shamelessly uses her any way he wants, this little pipsqueak who still pisses his pants and wets the bed, who still relies on his mother to tie his own shoelaces. Anyone who wants to confirm that what I'm saying is true needs only to stand outside our primary and secondary schools for a few minutes when people are coming and going, and I swear to God Almighty you'll hear things that will make you wish you never had a mother. The taxi driver who retired from public service five years ago sticks his ugly bald head out the window during the glorious month of Ramadan and insults the mother of the old man driving an SUV who wraps his head in a towel spotted with filth and grime. In a rage, the old man hurriedly curses the taxi driver's mother until the listener believes that she might just be—even if she's dead or very, very old—hanging out in that place of ill repute near Nahj Zarqoun that I don't want to mention by name because everybody knows it, including the people of Bin Qardan, al-Ala, Bourj al-Khadra, Beni Kheddache, Sajanan, and Talabat. Anyone who walks the streets of the capital or other cities listening to people of all ages and backgrounds as they curse and insult one another and get into fistfights or butt heads with each other will have no choice but to conclude that mothers are the root of all evil, responsible for all the sins and mistakes committed from the highest echelons down to the popular classes, that all mothers are like this or like that. Even someone who can only read sign language would understand. Our high school first-year Arabic teacher—a short, jolly-faced native of the Jerid region with a light heart, a sharp tongue, and small cunning eyes like those of a fox waiting for the opportunity to attack the henhouse when the family isn't looking—used to enjoy reminding us almost every day how the Jerid had produced great men, legal scholars, judges, lawyers, writers, and poets. It's enough that the region produced Abu al-Qasim al-Shabi. Then he would close his beady little eyes and begin to recite his famous poem: "If, one day, the people desire to live, then fate must respond."

Ahh, that time seems so distant now . . .

The newspapers were interested in my case from the very beginning right up until the bitter end, so it wasn't odd for the courtroom to be filled with such a crowd, teeming with women and men who were fired up and eager to know what destiny had in store for me after having appalled millions of people by what my hands had perpetrated on a hot summer day out in that ravine, where I didn't hear anything but the chirping of cicadas. I think it was natural for all their stares to fall upon me as the verdict was read out, searching for the expressions that would appear on my face, which might reveal what sort of emotions and excitements and feelings were coursing through me. But this huge mass of men and women must have felt great disappointment because they couldn't possibly have seen anything in my features resembling remorse or fear. Instead I may have even cracked a crooked smile upon hearing the verdict just so that they would know how absolutely satisfied I was with the outcome. They stared back at me, as astonished as clowns. Meanwhile that smug, plump, older woman in a black dress who had attended every court session as if the matter concerned her personally began to grumble angrily to herself as something washed over her long, pale face, the face of a decrepit old nag, something indicating her readiness to pounce on me and teach me one final lesson before I drifted away into the eternal darkness. Could it be that the verdict handed down against me wasn't enough to satisfy her thirst for revenge? Maybe I had defied all of this woman's expectations, maybe she had been waiting for me to burst out crying from remorse over what I had done, so that she could go home at peace in order to instruct her children and her grandchildren about how the young man who had committed that heinous crime they read all about in the magazines and newspapers had broken down in the end, had cried in agony in front of the judges and the lawyers and the packed audience in the courtroom when he finally understood that what he had done was an act of the wicked Devil and not the act of someone who believes there is one true God and that loving one's mother is one of His commandments.

The court reporter was also outraged and started making me nervous with his fiery glances, as if he wanted to yell at me that the verdict handed down in my case was too lenient, and how if he had been in the judge's shoes he would have immediately started a fire right there inside the courtroom and thrown me into the inferno. The truth of the matter is that this misshapen, ashen-faced, middle-aged man with worm-eaten teeth had despised me from the very first session, and I hated him with equal measure. He seemed to be one of those people who pretend to be chaste, truthful in speech, sincere in action, and noble in their dealings with others, but who turn out, in fact, to be savage beasts that would tear the teeth out of a barking dog. My affable lawyer was blessed with the friendliness of a spinster who still hopes to get married in spite of the fact that she is over forty years old and lives in a country where the most recent official census has confirmed there are more women than men. He whispered something to me I couldn't totally comprehend, something about a presidential pardon. But I didn't respond. I wanted to be taken away to the prison cell as soon as possible. That's all I really wanted!

11

THE MOTHER

It's better if I start with my mother. My mother—may God have mercy upon her—who used to tell me I was born in a hard year, one that was destabilized by upheavals and painful events. The earth was parched, the water wells had run dry, and the olive and almond trees were all shriveled up. Famine had begun to threaten the country. Despite the sacks of flour the state provided for the needy, many people would go to sleep hungry. My mother also used to tell me how in the hotter-than-average summer of the year I was born, military vehicles showed up and motored around like crazy in our village and neighboring regions in order to haul young men off to Bizerte to fight in the war that had broken out against the French. Bashir, my maternal Aunt Warda's eldest son, was one of them. According to my mother, Aunt Warda, and a number of other relatives, everybody adored him for his good manners, his kind heart, and his pleasing appearance. He had only just mustered up the courage to ask a young woman he was in love with for her hand in marriage when they carted him away to Bizerte. One day after he arrived there he was killed by a bullet to his head and buried there along with many others. Our family mourned him for a long time, and Aunt Warda nearly lost her mind from the tragedy. My mother used to claim that the leaders and anyone with connections to the state in our village were overjoyed because we had offered up a martyr to the Battle of Bizerte and God would now grace the village with rain and abundant good fortune and the satisfaction of important people in the capital. The other misfortune that befell us that year was the death of my uncle Omar, my mother's younger brother, in a car accident in Sousse. He had gone there looking for work. But crossing the street downtown at sunset a truck ran him over and killed him instantly. When I got older, my mother told me how she remained in mourning out of grief over his death until I was a year old. From time to time, with a grave face that preserved her classic beauty until the last day of her life, and as dark shadows of profound sadness continued to haunt her soul, she would tell me, "My daughter, you were born in a barren, black year. I pray to God, glory and praises be upon Him, that He won't bring it upon us ever again or upon any part of the Muslim umma!"

As for my father—may God also have mercy upon him—he didn't have much of a presence in the house compared to my mother, who was so ubiquitous that nothing could ever be done without her approval and consent. I can't remember my father ever doing anything large or small without consulting her first. He was her blindly obedient disciple who never dared to oppose her or disagree with her, even when she was wrong. He would remain perfectly content as long as she was pleased with him, and he would flit away in joy with so much as a smile from her. When she got angry or her features took on a glowering expression and her eyes got all red, he'd slink away and wouldn't come back home until he was certain her bad mood had passed. Aunt Warda started taking a keen interest in me that aroused the jealousy of my three sisters. She told me that the beauty God had bestowed on my mother had caused a lot of problems for her when she was younger. From the age of fourteen the men in our village as well as in neighboring villages started hovering around her like relentless flies. Every one of them wanted her for his bride and was prepared to offer the best they had in order to win her, but she wasn't interested in any of them. Not a single one ever received a kind word or a glance or a smile from her. In fact, during that time when there were so many suitors asking for her hand, my mother fell in love with a young man who was famous for his wealth and charm and his talent for hunting and horseback riding, but she concealed her love from her family and didn't speak of it to anyone except for Aunt Warda. Just as she was on the verge of revealing everything in order to silence the tongues that had begun to spin rumors all around her, an early autumn flash flood following torrential rains in the Maraq al-Layl Valley swept her beloved away. Aunt Warda says that her sister Zeina (that's my mother's name) didn't shed a single tear, but drowned instead in a sorrow as black as tar, cut herself off from people, and stared at those who interrupted her solitude as though she were on the brink of madness. From time to time, she would be seen wandering around aimlessly in the fields or the almond and olive groves, eyes adrift, hair disheveled, her face all pale. Over the course of many months nobody in the family dared to get near her or speak to her about anything.

Then one mellow evening, as the world was swimming in a splendid light, my mother duped my grandmother, calmly informing her that she wanted to get married to Salih, Hania's son. My grandmother was shocked; that is to say, she was mortified by the thought that her daughter, who had only rarely spoken to her for many months, had now started raving like someone on the verge of losing her grip on reality. And she was right to feel that way, at least, according to Aunt Warda. At that point, Salih, Hania's son, hadn't even asked for her hand yet. Rather, it's certain that he had never even thought of such a thing in the first place. As far as that poor, skinny, very shy and introverted young man was concerned, my mother was like the morning star—it was enough for him to contemplate her beauty from afar, knowing full well that getting any closer to her would be impossible. Besides, he was the sole breadwinner for his aging mother, who would begin to wheeze loudly after taking just a few steps because of her weak heart. On top of all that, Salih didn't possess any distinguishing features that would ever make a young woman who was as beautiful as my mother desire to marry him in the first place.

Uncertain of what to do, my grandmother left her daughter and hurried off in a panic to see my grandfather and apprise him of the strange proposal she had just heard. It didn't take long before my grandfather, who was well known for being quick-tempered, had gone out of his gourd, and the sparks shooting from his eyes made him seem capable of bringing the house down upon its foundation. Once she sensed that he had started to calm down, my grandmother returned home to see her daughter, hoping to hear something from her that might indicate that what she had said before was just a joke. Just a joke and nothing more. But my mother, in the same calm tone of voice, affirmed that she would refuse to marry anyone but Salih, Hania's son. Or else. "Or else what?" my grandmother furiously demanded from her. "Or else I'll do something terrible, something the people will never forget!" my mother yelled, her beautiful white face shining with clear defiance. As soon as word of this got out it preoccupied the people of the village for a long time. Some said that Zeina might have been bewitched by a cunning old woman who wanted to take revenge on her because of her beauty. Others spread the rumor that she must have been doing it just to have a laugh at everyone after those long months spent in silence and isolation. Then there were those who whispered here and there how she must have been cursed after refusing to marry the best men the village had to offer, and that God was going to exact a terrible revenge from her if she did marry Salih, Hania's son, because he wouldn't be able to satisfy her in bed or provide her with the comfortable life that every young lady of her beauty and household talents would expect. Salih vanished all of a sudden and some wicked tongues spread rumors about how he had fled from the terror of what he had heard, but some people who came back from Kairouan claimed to have seen him strolling through the markets that very morning, and in the afternoon somebody surprised him just as he was raising his arms in prayer at the shrine of Sidi al-Suhbi. So when he reappeared in the village decked out in a fancy qamariya robe, wearing a shashiya cap on his head and strutting around in black shoes that glinted in the sunlight, my maternal uncle Mukhtar decided to talk to him, with the intention of convincing his sister that her stubbornness was unhelpful and that her choice was unacceptable even for those involved. After listening to him for a long time, Salih smiled a childish grin, spread apart his hands and said, as the scents of Kairouan wafted off of him, "What's so strange about all of this, Si Mukhtar? I've loved Zeina ever since we were children, and she loves me as far as I can tell. So I think our marriage will be a blessing from God!"

Aunt Warda says that my mother's marriage to Salih, Hania's son, was truly that, because God blessed the people that year with a bountiful harvest of olives and almonds that kept the specter of poverty at bay. Therefore it wasn't strange for the wedding to last a full seven days and seven nights. And Ali, Khayra's son, who I had only ever known as an aging, worn-out, and somber old man, was at the peak of his fame and glory at the time. No wedding could be a success without him. Aunt Warda told me that at her sister Zeina's wedding he sang the sweetest and most beautiful songs, which not only delighted the men, women, and children, but also the horses and the trees and the silverware, even the foothills and Mount Tirzah. After being silent for a little while, Aunt Warda added, "Your mother may have made the right choice, because experience shows that marriage for love doesn't last. It leaves its participants with nothing but sorrow and pain. But rational marriage is usually successful and propitious, and blessed for those who choose it."

THE SON

The cops barged in on me while I was fast asleep in a Hammamat hotel that I can't remember the name of right now because I had shown up there drunk late at night and only just barely found my way to the room booked for me. By nine a.m., I was in custody in the capital. But first they had a taxi driver take us to the arches on the road to Zaghouan.

After staring at me for a long time the driver looked at the policemen circled around me one after another, and with absolute confidence in himself and in his memory, he nodded his head repeatedly as proof that I was the one they were looking for. Then he turned his face away with the pride of someone who has succeeded in the task he had been assigned. Maybe they thought I was going to try every trick in the book and every means possible to deny the charge they meant to lay on me, because they started getting all puffed up like furious devils that would smash my face in if I tried any funny stuff instead of answering their questions. But with utter composure and calm I told them, "Please excuse me, gentlemen, there's no need for you to beat me up or smash my face in because I'm fully prepared to answer any question you care to ask me, of whatever sort. What's more, in order to avoid wasting time and energy and getting on people's nerves, I'm ready to dictate my confession to you in full, without any detours or evasions. That's right, I'll do that for you, respected sirs, so just calm down and hear me out." They were astonished and continued to stare at me with doubt and suspicion, convinced I was setting some sort of a trap they hadn't caught on to yet. In order to assure them

16

that I was quite serious about what I had said, I actually started to narrate everything that had happened with the utmost precision.

The truth is that from the moment the fire broke out in the ravine I intended to give myself up to the first police patrol I saw as I made my way back to the capital on foot, but I put it off and went home instead, as if I simply had to see it in whatever condition it was after finally carrying out what I had been planning for many months. As soon as I got home I took a cold shower that invigorated me and gave me back some of the mental clarity that had evaporated during that infernal afternoon. Afterward I began searching here and there for something, I wasn't sure what exactly, when all of a sudden I found more than 2,500 dinars in my large closet. In that moment I told myself it would be such a shame for me to enter the gloom of prison and then go on to face the gallows without ever getting my hands on some of the things I had always dreamed of. I immediately took a taxi to Bab al-Bahr, where I had only ever been when I was broke or just about. After the cab dropped me in front of the Municipal Theatre I headed toward a store in the Palmarium where I bought two robes, two high quality summer shirts, and a nice pair of shoes. Then I got my hair cut in the latest style on Carthage Street. From a perfume shop in Colisée I bought some expensive cologne that the attractive saleswoman who looked like a model assured me had been specially designed for young men my age. Putting all of that into a leather satchel I had also bought in a shop in Colisée, I headed toward Muncef Bey Station to hire a private car that would take me to Sousse. By six p.m. I was strutting around on the beach at Bu Jaafar like a prince, with a jasmine flower over my left ear, my eyes on the pretty girls as I searched for one who could make me forget all about the pitch-black shadows of that awful day, which was like nothing I had ever experienced in my life before. It was clear to me from the start that my southern friend Aziz had been right when he told me how the girls in Sousse during the summertime are like worms wriggling through the earth after the autumn rains. Whichever way you turned, one might wound you with her deadly charms. With this one it's her black or bluish-black or blue eyes, with that one it's her short boyish hair, with another it's her prominent chest that nearly pops right out of her see-through shirt, with a fourth it's her pleasantly sexy gasp, with a fifth it's her ass that lights a fire inside your body until you feel as though you're burning up, with a sixth it's her belly button that appears to be drawn clearly at the top of her pants, and with another it's her way of walking to the beat of the song, "Bend over, little deer, bend over." Another one tells you with every move she makes how badly she hungers for your thing, to the point that you get so horny and bursting with passion that you're unable to stand still. Every color, O generous woman, give me what you got . . . ahh . . . ahhh . . . aaaaaaah. O night, O eye. I raced like a madman from one to the next, smiling at all of them, treating them gently with sweet words I had learned mostly from movies and TV. My hunt didn't last long, though, because I was with her when the clock struck eight. My God, my God. What a blessing—she was just my type. Her name was Zumurda. She was from Kairouan and came to Sousse every season because it's her favorite city. It's true that she had been to Hammamat and Nabeul and Manastir and the capital and many other places but Sousse was her favorite. Zumurda said she was a secretary but I knew she was lying. Something unmistakable about her marked her as one of those women whose only job in the summertime is to cruise for men on the beach at Bu Jaafar or at one of the big hotels. Whatever. The important thing was for me to spend one unforgettable night with her, and to hell with her after that! Besides, I had lied to her, too. I told her I was an engineering student from a wealthy family in Carthage. If I had been honest and told her that I was from that dirt-poor village in the woods of Kairouan at the western foot of Mount Tirzah she would have run away from me in a panic as soon as possible. Ahh. Lying is always useful in this country. People say that lying is some kind of monstrous act and that liars are going straight to hell without any mercy or pity, but everybody in this country lies, making an art form of it in a way that is unlike any other people in the world that I am aware of.

After strolling along the beach at Bu Jaafar together for half an hour I invited Zumurda to a restaurant. We ate delicious fish and I drank three beers. Afterward we hopped in a taxi that took us to a hotel disco she knew. We danced for more than two hours, then we went for a walk on the beach that was nearly empty because it was so late. Just then, we plunged into torrid kisses, but fearing that we might get caught in the act by some "night demons" we agreed I would get a room for her and one for me back at the same hotel where we had gone dancing. And that's what actually happened, although I must confess that up until that night I hadn't been entirely confident in my manhood. Previous experiences had left me feeling disgraced and ashamed of myself. For example, this one time, my friend Aziz, who has a bigger heart than any of my other friends (who you can count on one hand), came into a bit of money and invited me to spend the weekend with him in Hammamat. We booked a room in a nondescript hotel near the entrance to the city. After dinner we went out to a nightclub, started drinking beer and flirting with girls. Without trying very hard we caught two olive-skinned young ladies who looked so much alike they could have been twins. After a short walk down by the beach each one of us went off with his new friend. My new girlfriend was named Naima, I think. It was a warm fall night, the stars were twinkling in the sky and there was nobody else around. At least that's how we imagined things were. As soon as her soft little hand touched my body it stood up all engorged. She was mesmerized and stroked it a little with her hand, then whispered as her body yielded and grew more and more pliant, "Stick it in, quickly, please. Stick it in. I can't wait any longer!" Upon hearing her whisper those words I felt as if someone had poured cold water all over me when I wasn't looking. And just like that the fire that had been scorching my body was extinguished, and it went limp and shrank down to the size of a fava bean! She tried to grow it back to its former state, with kisses at first, then with caresses and dirty talk, but it stayed like that, unaffected by what she was doing or saying. She cast me a contemptuous glare I haven't forgotten until this very moment and then hurriedly stormed off in the direction of the nightclub. I ran after her but she shouted in my face, "Don't come near me before making sure you're a real man!" I was hurt by what she said and I went back to the hotel scatterbrained and disoriented only to fall into a deep sleep punctuated by terrifying nightmares. The next day I discovered that the one I think is named Naima told Aziz everything that had happened and he avoided looking at me for several days.

I had bitter experiences with other girls and the scenario was always so similar that some of my friends started to whisper among themselves that I might be impotent. The very idea sent me into a panic. However, what gave me some comfort was the fact that whenever I was alone in bed, thinking about that girl sipping a cool drink in the Belvedere Garden or about another one who kept smiling at me on the Metro from Bab al-Asl Station to Republic Square, or about that other one I followed through the crowd at the al-Qarana market, I'd come in absolute pleasure, doing it five or even six times without getting bored or stopping to eat. I have as many fantasies about being with famous actresses as I have hairs on my head. Egyptians, Lebanese, Turks, French, Italians, Americans — they all come obediently into my cold bed at night, where they ignite a roaring fire that doesn't die down until the white line of dawn becomes discernible from the blackness of night. I undress them in my imagination and then have my way with them. My favorite is that French-Algerian woman. I get especially turned on whenever she cries, and I long to be there beside her, to comfort her and dry her tears. Or that blonde American with short hair and a perfect ass who plays the role of the young wife cheating on her rich older husband with an unkempt young man who doesn't even have enough money to pay for dinner—she's my heart's delight. I can't get that scene out of my mind in which we screw on the dinner table late at night while the duped husband loudly snores away. Even Princess Diana, may God bless her and install her in the paradises of His heavens, couldn't escape me. I did it with her a number of times before she died in that tragic accident in the Paris tunnel. But whenever I found myself face to face with a real girl my fire would always go out and "he" would betray me, leaving me there to wade through the remains of my disappointment and inadequacy, so it was only natural for me to go to bed with Zumurda that night with my fingers crossed. I managed to do it with her once, a second, and a third time. How long could I keep this up? She screamed and hollered as I pounded and pounded and pounded away until I imagined that all of Sousse could hear her, and what I was doing to her. We went on and on like that. Before drifting off to sleep we did it once more standing up, our faces turned toward the sea, which looked purple and green in the breaking dawn.

We woke up at eleven. In the shower I thought about how a talented hunter wouldn't be satisfied with just one catch. So I lied to Zumurda and told her my father was leaving the next morning for Rome and that I had to get back to Carthage right away. Then I gave her twenty dinars and set off for Manastir. By the end of that evening I had caught this Dutch cow who was more than ten years older than me, though seeing her ass jiggle with every step she took made me overlook the difference in age between us. Maybe because that Dutch heifer was so happy to wind up with an olive-skinned young man like me, who was younger than her to boot, she spoiled me rotten that night. She invited me to dinner at a fancy restaurant, where we had two glasses of red wine, and then she went on to drink two glasses of cognac by herself. Afterward she booked me a room in the same hotel where she was staying. I learned new positions from her on that crazy night, which made me more confident in my own masculinity. I left Manastir armed with that new knowledge and headed to Hammamat, where I arrived at noon. I dropped my suitcase off in a small hotel and then went down to the beach. I went swimming for more than two hours and strolled along the shore until I approached South Hammamat. Then I went back to the hotel. I took a shower and fell asleep until seven. I had some very bad grilled lamb for dinner and then headed out to that same nightclub where I had gone with my friend Aziz, praying to God that I would run into that woman I think is named Naima so I could show her what those who come from rough villages do to girls who complain about their manhood. God didn't hear my prayer so I got annoyed. Trying to get rid of that feeling I started chugging beers, my eyes on the door. At exactly eleven o'clock, the one I think is named Naima came in with her friend who looks just like her. At that moment, my anxiety disappeared and the flame of desire was sparked in my body once again.

At first the two of them avoided me, they ignored my presence, but I soon persuaded them to join me. It was easy once the two of them noticed how I was throwing money around. As we walked down onto the dance floor, her chest pressed against mine and her lips touched my cheek. I whispered to the one I think is named Naima that I was going to let her taste something she'd never had before. At that moment she pulled in closer to me and started stroking it with her warm hand until I couldn't take it any more and we slipped into the garden to do it for the first time standing up. Then we finished up in the hotel where I was staying. I didn't leave her until she had squealed twice with pleasure. Was it because of the monstrous act I had committed that my friend regained his vitality and no longer betrayed me like he used to do in the past?

I woke up around noon and found a letter from the one I think is named Naima informing me that she'd be waiting for me at the nightclub around the same time as the night before. But I didn't want her anymore. So after ten I started cruising around from one nightclub to the next. In each one I drank a beer or two. I finally went back to the hotel at nine the next morning, flying somewhere between heaven and earth, with dreams and thoughts flickering in my head like the stars above. When I opened my eyes those towering bodies filled my tiny room and their eyes communicated their readiness to bash my head in if I showed the slightest sign of obstinacy or resistance.

THE MOTHER

Now I'm neither dust nor a clump of ash. I'm that little girl they named Najma, which means star, possibly because I was born in the middle of the summer, at that moment when night is just starting to divide from day and when the morning star shines with its marvelous light that has enticed travelers through empty desolate lands. From the very beginning they used to say I was the spitting image of my mother. So my grandmother would sigh deeply from time to time and then whisper, as if talking to herself, "I hope to God she doesn't turn out as stubborn and sharp-tongued as her mother!" But God didn't heed her prayer, and I turned out even more stubborn and sharp-tongued than her. While the other girls my age and even those who were a bit older than me liked to play and spend time together at each other's homes or out in sandy riverbeds, I always preferred being around and playing with boys. I usually beat them at their own games. While most people were taking their afternoon naps that put them out of commission, when nothing can be heard but the chirping of cicadas, I'd sneak away with them unnoticed, out into the almond or fig groves. On both moonlit and shadowy nights I'd stay up late with them playing hide-and-seek, which I liked better than all the other games because it allowed me to touch a boy's supple warm body and to feel those places that would make me yearn for him to put his thing—that thus far only my hand had grazed—into my lap, to give me a kiss and perhaps to do other things to me that weren't even clear yet in my mind. In early fall, when the heat eases up and the weather gets nicer,

I used to go with the village children on that long arduous journey up to Mount Tirzah, which stood out there to the east, tall and bare. I'd climb up with them to the highest peak in order to see the view, enchanted by the plains of Hajeb El Ayoun, al-Hawarib, and al-Shabika, and the green spaces along the banks of the Maraq al-Layl Valley. On clear autumn days we hoped to be able to catch a glimpse of the minarets of the Kairouan Great Mosque or anything that might convince us that the City of God wasn't very far away from us, that we were right near the gates of the city that had been built by the companions of the Prophet amid the salt marshes in the arid desert. Our elders all used to say that making pilgrimage there is comparable to completing the hajj to Mecca. Then we'd turn toward the north and see Mount Ousselat staring right back at us, also tall and bare. Along its base the Ousselati plains looked red because the tilling and planting season had just begun. Our imaginations would carry us even further away as we imagined the capital, which might have been just beyond that faint line where sky clings to earth, from where travelers in our family used to return all bewildered in their movements and their speech, as absent-minded as if they had just received a swift kick to the head. Mount Kasra was to the west, and the village that could be seen on its peak looked like a giant egg. To its left the forests of Fajj al-Akhal extend out as black as the tar that is found there. At that moment unease seeped into our hearts and an icy chill spread through our bodies as we remembered the horror stories our elders would tell us about bandits and people whose throats got slit from ear to ear, about others whose possessions and animals were stolen from them, whose clothes were torn right off their bodies and who were left naked in the darkness of the cold desolate night as famished wolves howled nearby. Between Fajj al-Akhal and our village are the Masyute foothills, which looked as red as a big scalped head. The elders say it was a volcano in ancient times. Beyond all of that are Maktar and al-Kef and then Algeria. According to our family lore, the Gharaba tribe arrived on the backs of their black mules, their eyes all red from exertion and exhaustion, with dust hanging off their black or gray beards after an arduous journey across arid deserts and craggy mountains. They came making oaths to God and His Prophet and the holy saints, singing songs and religious hymns to the beat of the bendir drum. They had come to prove that their magic and spell casting were capable of making barren women fertile, of marrying off the most unmarriageable girls, of exorcising devils and jinns, of restoring youthfulness to those who had lost it and of opening the gate of sustenance for those with bad luck or whom the eye of God had forsaken. My grandfather was among the few who were convinced that they were nothing but swindlers and charlatans who secretly brought with them evil deeds that affront morals and religion, so he would stubbornly drive them away every time they tried to come near our house. To the south were Mount Maghilla and the Sbeitla plains, where gunshots could be heard over ululations, where dark-skinned men marched to their deaths in the bare mountains or on the edges of the desert, silent, composed, intent on revenge because blood can only be avenged by more blood.

In the winter I used to crawl underneath warm blankets with boys and my body would cling to theirs as we listened to the wondrous tales our elders told around the fire, tales that quickly whisked us off to sleep, accompanied by the heroes from those stories about men, jinns and demons, ghouls and birds, and one-of-a-kind creatures that could speak every language, cunning and deceptive, always setting traps and often prevailing over humans. I continued doing that until my breasts had developed. From that point on, my grandmother started prodding my mother to keep a closer watch on me, from the moment I woke up in the morning until I returned to bed at night, so that I wouldn't cause any scandals that my family would have to suffer the consequences up until Judgment Day, as she used to say.

My favorite day in our village was Thursday, the day of the weekly market, when hordes of people from every province would descend upon us. From the moment the rooster started crowing, announcing the approach of daybreak, until just before the sun appeared, noise and shouting increased as the people's voices got all jumbled together and grew louder and louder, until I was unable to make out what they were saying. As soon as I left the house I'd find our village overflowing not only with men, women, and children, but also with donkeys, mules, camels, cows, lambs, ewes, goats, chickens, rabbits, and piles of eggs; cars and trucks slowly forced their way through the dense crowds, buses honked after every ten meters, and tractors kicked up clouds of dust that made it hard to breathe; Bedouins with scorched faces and red eyes stared all around with suspicion and caution, elderly men crept along at a snail's pace, children joked around and hollered, water-sellers hurried past with black water skins on their backs shouting, "Cool off, thirsty ones, cool off"; barefoot and half-naked mendicants moaned and writhed and begged as unbearable humiliation ran across their faces. Women from Jerir and Amsha walked around brazenly, raising their voices without any shame or embarrassment, unaffected by all those men around them. My grandmother would pinch me or the woman next to her and whisper, aghast, "Look at how they mix with men, without any shame or modesty. May God protect us and keep us from evil and misfortune!" A man like a burnt column quivering from the intensity of his hunger stood in front of a stand that sold savory pastries, as saliva oozed from his thick filthy beard. My grandmother said that Muhammad al-Bouhali lost his mind after losing a large sum of money gambling one night and was forced to sell his small olive orchard—the last thing he owned. He stumbled around in rags, laughing sometimes, at other times cursing the heavens and the earth and the day when women started dragging men around by their ears all pathetic and humiliated. As I took in all of these sights, I wanted to inscribe everything I was hearing and seeing in my memory. There was a tall, skinny black man wearing flowing pants with his head wrapped in a white turban who smiled at me once and revealed large gleaming-white teeth. I recoiled from him in panic and clung to my grandmother who I was with in the vegetable market. But he continued to smile at me, even made a gesture to convey what a pretty and well-behaved girl I was, and I immediately buried my face in my grandmother's purple robe. When I opened my eyes he had vanished. Sometime later I would discover that he was none other than Abdel Hafiz, who the people of the village and all the surrounding areas used to adore for his dancing skills and his superior ability to enliven weddings and parties. I would even develop a crush on him, becoming just another one of those girls enthralled by his dancing and his singing. When he died of a heart attack, I was in the capital and I made sure to attend his funeral, where I cried warm tears.

I was ten years old when I visited Kairouan for the first time, accompanying my grandmother who was leading an annual pilgrimage to the shrine of Sidi al-Suhbi. We stayed there for one day and one night. After we returned, I spent weeks and weeks walking around, eating, talking, and sleeping as the marvelous sights I had seen in the City of God passed through my mind one after another.

THE SON

I forgot to mention that while I was sipping my coffee at Hammamat Bay late in the afternoon on the day before I was arrested I heard an old man telling a young man about a torched corpse found by a shepherd out in a ravine not far from the Arches of Zaghouan. The old man, as red-faced as a European and wearing a swish white robe, commented, "Something like that, Rafiq my boy, is unmistakable proof that people are turning into wild beasts. No morals. No religion. Nothing of the sort anymore. Just robbing and looting and thievery and trickery. Corruption's getting worse from one day to the next. Scandalous crimes like this one in the papers every day means there's no longer any place in this difficult time for people with a shred of common decency!" The fair-skinned young man, dressed in jeans, a white shirt and light-weight black shoes, and with black Ray-Ban sunglasses covering his eyes, replied with a smile on his lips, "Listen, my dear uncle. Shocking crimes don't just happen here, but in every country on earth. I don't think it has anything to do with the existence of common decency or lack thereof. One day I read a news story about an Arab woman who killed her husband and then ate his heart raw out of revenge after he betrayed her with her younger cousin. Now, let's forget all about this matter, why don't you join me this evening for a flamenco concert at the International Theater."

"Thank you very much," the old man replied, and then added, "That would be nice. I love flamenco and everything from Spain. I've been there five times you know, and I still have fond memories of the place and its people, especially the people of al-Andalus!" And so the old man and the young man quickly forgot all about the torched corpse and became wrapped up in a stimulating conversation about flamenco and malouf, then about the tourist season and the exorbitant prices, especially in restaurants and hotels, and about the Algerians and Libyans who overrun the city. The truth of the matter is that I wasn't at all interested in their conversation about the smoldering corpse, as if the matter didn't concern me at all. As if the crime I had committed on a day in which the whole world— its people and spirits, devils and angels, animals and insects, everything in it, whether moving or still—boiled like a kettle from the searing heat was the work of another human being, someone who hadn't been identified yet, not only to everyone else but to me as well. This wasn't strange. Ever since the act I had been planning for so long had finally been accomplished, I became another creature altogether. A creature completely disconnected from who I was before. A creature that desires to fly high up in the sky like all the happy free birds, to dance until morning and eat his fill of fresh meat that had been forbidden to him for many years, to give water to his feeble, thirsting little friend that had sufficed with whatever affection and tender strokes his own hand would lavish upon him during the solitude of bitter cold nights, and then to just get so drunk that sea would become dry land and dry land would become sea, that trees would turn into giraffes, elephants, wild cows, and other strange animals like those I used to see in the Belvedere Garden.

By that afternoon, I had mustered up the strength to head down to Djerba to spend a few days and nights with those blonde German women who flock there in huge numbers, according to local rumor, because the men in their home country are so cold. Everyone who has ever tasted their honey affirms how truly phenomenal they are in bed, from the front and from the rear until the rooster's crow. From there I'll go on to walk through the oases of Tozeur and Nefta and Douz before heading deeper into the desert. I'll cross the border with smugglers until I arrive in the land of the Touareg, and I'll wear a black veil and a blue caftan like they do, ride on a white camel and drift aimlessly through the desert that stretches out endlessly in all directions, from Niger to Sudan, through Algeria, Libya, and Chad. As time passes the sun will tan my skin, and I'll become one of them, forgetting all about the creature I once was, and the people of my country will forget all about me too, to the point that there will no longer be a single trace of me left in their memory, or perhaps I might get transformed on their tongues into a thrilling story that amuses them at their late-night soirees and get-togethers. That's right, that's what I was thinking about. From time to time I'd also think about an American film I had watched a year before my crime and which might have been a factor that drove me to do it. The hero of the film is an unemployed young man who is always wearing jeans and a denim jacket and who spends his time aimlessly wandering around a small, deserted, almost lonesome town. Then he falls in love with this blonde girl who is also strange looking and eccentric. One day he goes to see her father, a painter, to ask his permission to marry her, but the father flies into a rage and threatens to call the police if he doesn't get out of his house at once. With utter calm and self-confidence, the young man tells him, "If you do that, I'll kill you!" Unaffected, the painter hurries over to the telephone to follow through on his threat. At that moment, the young man pulls a gun out of his jacket pocket and shoots him dead. The girl feels no sorrow and doesn't get upset. Instead she follows the young man out into the forest and they live together in the wild for several weeks. One day the police nab her but the young man manages to kill them all. Then he goes on the lam with his girlfriend, running from place to place, from town to town, as the police, armed to the teeth, pursue them day and night. He killed anyone who got in his way, anyone who doubted him, whether it was a small child or an old man, even someone who was disabled or sick. He'd do it without pity and without mercy. The heroine watched him in silence, not once showing the slightest opposition to the awful things he's done. Now I must admit that I was so attracted to that young man that I started wishing to be like him, always moving forward, blowing the head off of anyone who got in my way. I'd continue on like that that until I reached the end of the earth, down at the bottom of the Dark Continent.

That's what I was thinking about as the summer night descended, soft and warm, and the sea shimmered with the colors of the sky at sunset—blood red and magenta, honey-yellow and dark gray, purple and blackish-blue. The crowds became more and more active. Blonde tourist girls walked around half-naked as olive-skinned young men ran after them with their eyes aglow from the intensity of their hunger for sex and pleasure. All of Hammamat quaked feverishly, perfumed with the aromas of jasmine, waiting for the night and the unrestrained delights and pleasures it would offer to those who desired them.

THE MOTHER

I was older, and our village was changing at an astonishing speed. Girls began going to school as if it were the most natural thing to do and nobody tried to stop them. Even those who were known for their extreme conservatism and for their staunch refusal to let women out of the house lowered their heads and remained submissively silent in the face of all the new things that suddenly intruded into their lives. Radio infiltrated most houses, putting an end to the long chatting soirees that were filled with stories and tales told by elders. As a result, all of those cities that once waved at us as if from the ends of the earth drew nearer, and by way of those broadcast programs we were able to hear people from there talk about their concerns and their joys, about the songs they loved, and about the hopes and dreams they wished would come true, which made us feel that they were no longer as far away from us or as different from us as they had once seemed. And thanks to the radio, too, the world around us grew in a tremendous expansion, and we were astonished to discover that there were many countries in the world, with names and capitals and kings and presidents that were hard for us to pronounce. By and by, as those hideous wooden shops were abandoned by their owners to fill up with filth, they started to disappear and clean stores with white walls and blue doors sprang up in their place. Powerful state officials began visiting our village so they could lecture the people for a long time about something they called "mutual aid," promising us a better life and a sunny future in which poverty and hunger and ignorance would disappear, in which the fortunes of the rich and poor would be leveled out. Perhaps because they felt that their time had passed and that there was no turning back and that the world to which they once belonged had begun to fall apart, wilting before their very eyes, the elderly seemed like they were hurrying to pass away before their fated time, as their faces had grown more wrinkled and more sorrowful with their frightened stares and their aversion to talking or even moving. Only my grandfather managed to retain some of his old dignity and that nimbleness he had been known for since he was a young man. He would continue to raise his voice, loud and defiant, cursing anyone who would refuse his orders or advice, and anyone who didn't behave properly or who strayed from the straight path, as if he wanted to verify his existence in a world that no longer noticed him. As for my grandmother, she watched these new developments with a kind of childlike curiosity, and unlike other people of her age she struggled to keep up and adapt. She'd listen to the radio a lot even when she couldn't understand what was being said. One time everybody had a long hard laugh when she asked, "But how can all those people who are always talking and singing and making speeches live inside the same little box?"

Although I was a lazy student who was hopeless in most subjects, especially math and spelling, I loved school from the very beginning. I loved it because it afforded me the opportunity to be freer than I was before and allowed me to hang out with boys all day long, to play the games we all wanted to play. Usually we'd do that when we got home from school at the end of the afternoon. During that time we'd forget everything around us, and continue playing and running around together through the dusty alleyways, singing and laughing loudly until we were stopped by the night. When I came home late, my grandmother punished me and my mother scolded me on more than one occasion, but I wasn't bothered by that, and I kept on playing and hanging out with the boys while the other girls would hurry home as soon as classes let out.

As I said, I used to love being around boys, yearning for them to listen to me, to do my bidding, to take into account whatever I said and recommended, just like al-Jazya al-Hilaliya with her tribesmen. My grandmother never got tired of telling the story of al-Jazya al-Hilaliya and I used to dream of being like her when I grew up. Men would ferociously fight one another just to win me while I sat cross-legged in the tent with my female servants, and my coal-black hair cascaded down to my waist as my heart thumped with love for the victorious warrior who deserved to have me as his reward.

I was the favorite of all the boys, those who were my age and even those who were older than me. My hanging out with them tempted them, as did my participation with them in everything they did in private and in public. For the most part I showed great talent in the games that mattered to them. That strengthened my influence and power among them. It was clear that every one of them wanted me to be for him and him alone. And out of jealousy, fierce battles would break out between this one or that one from time to time. But as soon as I intervened it would die out as quickly as it had been sparked, except I rarely did that because it used to appease my arrogance and my vanity to see them brawling over me and because of me, before they had even reached legal age, while I was still a little girl playing in the sand, one who hadn't even sprouted breasts yet.

But that night, I cried in anguish, and remained in pain and agony for days and nights on end because I had been forbidden from hanging out with the kids and attending the first screening of a movie in our village. I remember how we were coming back from school late in the afternoon when we saw a big olive-colored car advancing toward our village, and from it a loud voice could be heard announcing an evening screening that would begin at eight p.m. At that moment the kids got all excited and agitated, and something like a fever gripped the world all around us, to the point that I imagined that our village and all the farmyards around it had started to sway out of celebration for the happy event that was unlike anything the people had ever experienced before. In order to make sure that we would be on time, we ran home. I wolfed down my dinner, and ran for the door hurrying to get out as fast as I could, but my grandmother set up an obstacle in front of me. Brandishing a thick cane in my face, her face an angry expression like darkness in winter, she shouted at me, "And just where do you think you're going, you little bitch?"

I was confused and unable to respond. My grandmother brandished the thick stick in my face again and shouted, "Come on, out with it, or else I'll whip your hide with this stick!" "I want to go and see the movie!" I replied, nearly choking from the intensity of panic that gripped me because of the thick stick dangling in front of my face.

Without commenting, my grandmother shoved me back inside the house and called out to my mother, "Your daughter wants to go out and see a movie with boys tonight. We'll become a scandal on the tongues of those who do such things and those who don't!"

Anger consumed my mother and she slapped with me a strong blow that caused me to stagger backward as tears burned my eyes and cheeks. Suddenly, I found myself locked in a dark room and I broke down crying for a long time, even as the boys outside called everyone out into the village square. Afterward silence spread and I couldn't hear anything but the sound of dogs barking from time to time.

Sleep eluded me like a skittish bird. I opened the small window and stared up at the sky studded with stars until the entire village trembled with the commotion of people leaving at the end of the film. After nearly an hour, I slept the sleep of the deprived and the wretched of the earth.

THE SON

Contrary to what you might expect, I wasn't sad and didn't despair when I was arrested and thrown in jail. That might be attributed to the fact that for three straight days I had been satisfying some of my previously restrained and repressed desires. People in my country say that it's better for a person to live as a rooster for just one day than to be a chicken for an entire year. I was a virile rooster for three straight days, so now I can face the gallows at ease and at peace, without the slightest regret or sadness for the world I leave behind, with all its joys and sorrows, and without any remorse for the sins I have committed, quite the opposite of the two men who are with me on the cellblock who sob all the time because they received the same punishment. I know both of them very well because I shared the cells with them for many months.

The first one is named Ali, but his nickname is "Kaboura"—Knobby, probably because he's so stout and short. Despite his small size, though, he is respected for his exceptional ability to deceive and betray, in combat as well as in his daily interactions with other people. He is as sly as a fox and can never be trusted. Those who know him will say that he can defeat an opponent even when the latter is physically stronger. During the months I spent in jail with him, he would always boast about how he became friends with the actor Ali Chwerreb when he was young and how he saw him more than once quarrelling with police officers in Bab al-Khadra and Bab Suwayqa and Halfaouine and elsewhere. And because Ali Chwerreb had become one of his favorite actors, alongside the most famous Western movie stars like Lee Van Cleef, Charles Bronson, Clint Eastwood, and others, he would sometimes stay up very late at night, hidden out of his father's sight, just to catch a glimpse of Ali falling-down drunk, bumping into the wall on his right only to slam into the wall on his left in that narrow alleyway leading to the dilapidated house where he used to live with his elderly mother. He feared her the way he feared God and would obey her, therefore, with blind allegiance and without ever refusing a single demand. She was the only person who could tell him to shut up and make do so at once, the only person who could get him to obey the policemen's orders when their disputes were at their sharpest. Kaboura likes to give his lies free rein and claim that Sidi Ali (by which he meant Ali Chwerreb) used to reserve special affection for him, above all the other neighborhood kids, and would sometimes send him out to buy cigarettes and then once he had returned with them would stuff an entire week's pay in his pocket. He even once put his hand on his head and said, "I'm sure you're the only one·who can take my place in the neighborhood!" Kaboura swears with the most gullible conviction that "Sidi Ali" had said exactly that to him just one week before his death. One of his peers challenged him about it one evening after a long drinking session and Kaboura punched him once, knocking him to the ground where his head hit the pavement so hard that he died on the spot. At this point, Kaboura's eyes were bathed in tears as he said in a quavering voice that he was among those who accompanied Sidi Ali to his final resting place. The state-run press confirmed that more than one-third of the inhabitants of the capital were there, describing him as if he were a genuine national hero. I would laugh in secret whenever I heard talk like that out of the mouth of someone like Kaboura, because Ali Chwerreb, as several stories I heard about him both inside and outside of prison confirmed, was one of the most hardened, unscrupulous criminals. Up until that fatal whack on the pavement, Kaboura had never been good at anything in his gap-filled life except using his fists and drinking until he passed out. Nevertheless, many people in and out of the capital began talking about him as if he were in fact a genuine national hero who participated in building the new republic. It was clear from the scars and scratches that split open his pallid and malevolent face that Kaboura was what people call a "prison rat." Maybe he was like that ever since he came of age. He always likes to talk about the big-time criminals he came to know in his life, and with whom he had shared cells in the "European Tower" jail and the municipal prison in the capital, with great respect and esteem, placing above them a halo of glory, as if they were rebels who resisted French colonialism. He was very interested in the crimes committed by others, large or small, devoting lots of time to discussing them, stopping at their precise details, in the end handing down his own judicial opinions on their perpetrators in an attempt to make certain that his continuous frequenting of courtrooms and prisons had acquired for him some kind of unassailable expertise in the field of law. As for the crime that had finally brought him to death row, Kaboura wouldn't talk to anybody about it, that is, he wouldn't even mention it in passing. I learned about its details and circumstances from the others, and they used to do that out of his sight, avoiding his wrath. They say that Kaboura was close friends with another neighborhood kid who used to be a lot like him—stealing, beating people up, and mugging, strutting around Bab al-Bahr with a knife in his belt. But all of a sudden, that boy repented to God, and started to implement the recommendations of his mother, the Hajjeh, and started behaving respectably, beginning to earn a living from the sweat of his brow. With his hard-earned money, he built a house in one of those new neighborhoods connected to the Metro. He married a young lady from a wealthy family and they had two daughters and a son. Despite the fact that he had cut his connections with all his old wicked friends, he stayed in touch with Kaboura for some unfathomable reason. He used to invite him over to his house not only on harvests and holidays, but every other day and night as well, and together they stayed up late into the night. During times of hardship and difficulty, this friend didn't fail to help Kaboura or hesitate in doing so. When Kaboura went to jail, he would send a large gift basket along with his divorced sister. And with a decent amount of money, he would chip in for the cost of a defense lawyer, calling on his old friend to repent and reform himself. In spite of all that, Kaboura, who had suckled evil with his mother's milk, forgot about all of his friend's virtues and committed the monstrous deed that brought him to death row. One summer night, Kaboura wanted to stay up late with his friend, so he headed over to his house but he didn't find him there because his friend had gone away, his wife told him, to his hometown of Beja, to take care of something. On his way home, after polishing off two bottles of Koudia red wine in the Bab al-Khadra bar, Kaboura ran into his friend's son playing in the street, hugged him and kissed him as he always did, and then took his hand and told him, "Come walk around with your uncle

Kaboura in Bab Suwayqa, where he'll buy you a cold drink and then take you home in a taxi." The ten-year-old little boy agreed because Kaboura had been like an uncle to him, but the devil had spat his venom in Kaboura's soul, so he didn't want to back down from what he had planned to do ever since his lips touched the little boy's cheek. Instead of taking him to Bab Suwayqa, he led the little boy to a deserted shadowy place and, after gagging his mouth, raped him repeatedly. In the end, he strangled him to death, then dumped his body out in the open and went home and slept as though nothing had happened. The next morning, a municipal worker stumbled across the small boy's corpse and everyone rushed over to take a look, as the poor father wailed in horror. As for the mother, she passed out from the terror of shock and was immediately taken to the al-Rabita Hospital. That very same day, the security forces began their searches and investigations. It didn't take long. They gathered information from neighborhood children who saw the murdered boy on the night of the incident walking with a man whose description fit that of Kaboura. When the poor father learned that it was his old friend, whom he had treated with nothing but charity, who had tortured his child, he lost his mind and, barking like a dog, was taken to Manouba, where he spent half a year and came out afterward as though he had been stripped of his reason and his memory. When the judge handed down his ruling in the case, Kaboura fell apart, lost his swagger, his self-inflation, and his braggadocio to become a pathetic creature in the blink of an eye, sobbing almost all the time, not because he had murdered his friend's son in cold blood, but because he wasn't going to get out of jail this time around, to strut in front of the neighborhood children boasting how he was the rightful successor to Ali Chwerreb, and to show up at the Mezoued parties and dance until dawn to the beat of songs by Hedi Habbouba and Salah el Farzit, or to wander around the old and new neighborhoods in the capital with a knife in his belt, making a living off his girlfriend Houriya, whom he used to pimp out back in the good old days.

As for the second man on the cell block, he's named Saeed (Happy), but this name doesn't suit the man who has sobbed night and day ever since he was sentenced to death, and has started to recite the Quran, raising his voice loudly in prayer, beseeching God and His messenger to be compassionate and to forgive him for the sins he committed. He appears as though he came into the world weighed down with anxieties and sorrows and torments. All you have to do is look into his slightly dilated eyes and into his dry round face in order to see his tortured soul, as black as an abandoned well in the countryside. Not once have I seen him laugh or even smile. I don't think he did that even before he went to prison.

Saeed tends toward isolation and silence. From the moment he wakes up until the electric lights in the cells and the cellblocks are shut off, he is grave-faced, distracted, stumbling here and there, moving confusedly, chewing on his lips from time to time like someone who feels they've lost their life for no reason. Rarely does he join the other prisoners in conversations and chats. He absolutely never answers questions about his private life. As for other questions, he responds to them with extreme curtness, or else mutters something difficult to decipher. When responding to greetings, or inquiries concerning his health and psychological state or other such matters, he suffices with gestures.

Like Kaboura, Saeed avoids talking about the crime he committed, the one that brought him to death row, but most of the prisoners are as familiar with the events as if they had experienced them first-hand. Whenever they talk about it, you'd imagine they'd had a close relationship with Saeed, so much so that he no longer hid anything at all from them concerning his private life. In fact, some of them even delude themselves and others into believing they knew the color of his wife's underwear.

The facts show that Saeed was appointed as a teacher in a country in the Persian Gulf, and traveled there, leaving behind his wife and four-year-old daughter in the house he had built in the small town where he was born, nestled in the mountains in the northwest. His wife was an attractive woman, strong-willed. He fell in love with her after graduating from college, but she responded to his crazy love for her with loathing and disinterest. However, under pressure from her poor family, she was compelled to marry him, and at home she proceeded to treat him as though he were a lowly servant. That didn't bother him because his love for her was stronger than anything.

Upon his return from the Persian Gulf for summer vacation, the people of his town received Saeed coldly, dryly, as if he were a burdensome stranger who had come to disturb the serenity of their lives. Some faces frowning, others disgusted, doubtful, accusing, or scornful stares. Even those who would acknowledge him seemed to be doing so in spite of themselves. Humiliated and distressed and confused, Saeed arrived at his home only to be greeted by his wife with the same loathing and iciness, and on her face, which had grown more attractive, were expressions of distaste and resentment, as though he hadn't been away for a full nine months. The little girl who sat on his lap joyfully shouting "Baba! Baba! Baba!" wasn't able to return to his deeply wounded heart the delight that overflows upon returning to his family after a long absence.

His wife wasn't at all interested in the presents that Saeed began to shower upon her in an attempt to win back, if only a little bit, her love and tenderness. She responded to the questions he would ask her from time to time with extreme curtness, and her mind was distracted, in another land, distant, very distant. In that moment, he felt a painful twinge in the depths of his soul, and he started to sense that something dangerous had taken place in his absence, something that would soon demolish all those dreams and hopes that had propelled him to go into that arid desert country with the goal of accumulating enough money to make his little family happy. Running away from the face of his wife, who wouldn't even serve him a glass of water, Saeed went out into the street to find himself face to face with his younger brother. Distressed, he asked him, "What happened while I was away?"

"Come with me, I'll tell you everything," his younger brother replied.

In a private place far away from prying eyes, the younger brother related to his older brother how while he was away his wife had an affair with a young man from town who was studying law in the capital and who, before earning his baccalaureate, had been one of his students. Everyone in town knew that this young man was sleeping with his wife in their marital bed, that he was spending most of his time at her place when he came back from the capital on the weekend or on official holidays. He did it without any shame or fear of anybody. His wife would receive him all hunky-dory, within earshot and eyesight of everyone. Whenever he was with her, the house remained all lit up until late at night. Anyone who passed by there at night would hear the two of them shouting and whispering and saying shameful things. When both families tried to dissuade the unfaithful wife from her disgraceful actions, she turned red in anger and shouted, "I know what's best for me, so you all better just mind your own business and leave people alone to do what they want!" The younger brother added that most family members became too embarrassed to even set foot outside their houses, and wouldn't dare show their faces in front of the people in town. After letting out a deep sigh, the younger brother stared for a long time at the face of his older brother, who looked as though he had just been burned, and said, "My brother, this wife of yours is a disaster. I don't know how you're going to get rid of her!"

"Do you have a cigarette?" Saeed asked him.

"I do!" replied the younger brother, surprised because he knew his older brother to be a staunch opponent of smoking, and then handed him a cigarette and lit it for him.

Saeed took four consecutive drags, then flicked the cigarette away, and said in a loud voice as he rapidly walked away, "Tonight you'll see how I'm going to take care of her!"

Saeed went home. Without exchanging a single word with his wife, he got rid of his daughter who sat on his lap once again, and then took out a bottle of whiskey he had brought as a gift for a friend he had been close with ever since college and escaped into oblivion. Saeed, who had never drunk more than a few beers once in a while, and even then always at the urging of his friends, found his way that night to the last drop in the whiskey bottle, before going home to kill his wife and daughter while they snored soundly in a deep sleep. Afterward he wandered aimlessly through the countryside and the national guardsmen didn't find him until three days later. He was walking barefoot across thorny ground, his clothes torn, dusty-faced, and he was raving feverishly as spittle dribbled down his dusty beard and gray started to appear in his hair that had previously been jet-black.

THE MOTHER

I never got to see the film, but because the village children talked about it so much, I got to know its details from beginning to end. I won't deny the fact that some measure of vanity and self-importance overcame me when the children started whispering to me that in a few years I was going to be an exact replica of the actress who played the lead role in the Egyptian film they had watched on the back wall of our school. That's right, I'll be just like her. I'll have her stunning body, her beautiful eyes, her pleasant smile, her sexy gasp in moments of fear or confusion, her bouncy gait, her coyness and her flirtatiousness, and her tendency to toy with the hearts of her lovers. That's right, I'll have everything that Egyptian actress has, and people won't be able to tell us apart. I'll be vain and self-important, listening with pride and satisfaction to conversation that will spill out as sweet and pure as mountain spring water and to all the compliments that will be heaped upon me from right and left, from every direction, even as the other girls glance at me out of the corner of their eye and the fire of envy and jealousy burns their hearts out. I'll glance at them out of the corner of my eye, too, but with contempt, because they're dried-out, emaciated, dead-eyed, unconfident. As for me, I had already acquired a body whose feminine charms attracted the attention of men both young and old, never mind the fact that I wasn't even twelve years old yet. Whenever I was alone, my imagination would take me far, far away as I acted out the part of that Egyptian actress, seeing myself in love with the handsomest and noblest young man in the small dirt-poor village. He would love me back. He wouldn't be able to sleep, his mind wouldn't be at ease until he got a smile from me or a gesture or a word that I'd whisper to him one morning or one evening in the empty street as the eyes that never sleep and won't let anyone else sleep spy on us, monitoring our every move, the eyes of the old hags who practice occult magic and spit on the knots and the hypocritical old charlatans who pretend to be chaste and pious and godfearing and upright but in private are wicked, contemptuous creatures who do nothing but harm and insult others. One day, avoiding the shrewd eyes, I'd sneak away to the valley, out into the almond grove, where I'd have a rendezvous with my sweetheart. As soon as he touched my hand, my body would begin to tremble and a strange yet pleasurable fever I had never known before and would never know again would start to overcome me. When he pulled me in close to his chest, I would melt completely, forgetting who I was and where I came from. But the evil ones would quickly find us out and the dirt-poor village would shake like it does during a raging storm and the wicked tongues would start to spin false tales that spew their poisons everywhere. The hypocritical old men would raise their voices up high, begging God and His messenger and the holy saints to attack our love, to blow it away until there was nothing left but fragments. We'd be scared, cowering in shadowy corners, until one night my sweetheart would come to get me and we'd run off together to a distant land. Behind us the people of the dirt-poor village would hurl curses, brandishing rifles and sticks, even on that night, a pleasant fall night when the world is calm and still. From time to time, voices rise up here and there, but quickly quiet down and die out. For some reason I left the house and headed toward the almond grove. Maybe the magic of the evening drew me out. I was walking barefoot, my hair down over my shoulders, as night slowly fell, purple and soft. The birds retreated back into their nests, making their last peeps. I felt as though I were flying through air perfumed with the stunning scents of almond flowers. Just then, Yasin leaped out in front of me. In the faint purple darkness, he seemed taller than usual. Despite the many stories that people used to tell about his indecent behavior, especially toward young ladies, I didn't recoil from him, but stood my ground, confronting him instead. Without saying a single word to me, he unbuttoned his trousers and took it out. It was thick and black. I wasn't afraid this time. He drew closer to me. He grabbed my hand and started sliding it over it calmly, calmly over his thick black thing, with his eyes closed.

He continued doing that until he spurted sticky white fluid. Then he just left me standing there, my hand wet with that sticky white stuff, and disappeared into the darkness.

THE SON

They brought me dinner a few minutes ago, but I don't want to eat. Even if I tried, I would throw up the first bite before it ever reached my stomach. How can anyone who knows as I do that he no longer belongs to the world of the living crave food? It seems better for me to go on hunger strike so that they might then hurry this along and take me to the gallows before my appointed time, for fear that I may die a simple easy death, one that is unfitting for the abominable crime I perpetrated. As for Kaboura, it's sure that like a starving puppy he quickly and ferociously devoured whatever they threw his way, because he was still pulling for a miracle that would invalidate his death sentence. Or perhaps he is dreaming that luck might save him and bring him back once again to Halfaouine and Bab Suwayqa and Bab al-Bahr to beg for change and wander around like he used to do in the old days, a knife or two in his belt, and in his pocket a fistful of dinars that his lover, "The Daugher of Bab al-Fella," as he called her, presented him with every day. That's right, all of that is possible because Kaboura's impudence has no bounds. And Saeed, what do you think he did? Didn't he also wolf down his dinner that must have been revolting? I think he did or else he would have because I noticed over the course of the many months I spent with him how he epitomizes the most despicable kind of servility. He may hold advanced degrees, but he never dared to refuse an order. He was even afraid of the guards whom the prisoners turn into Karagöz shadow puppets, and in front of them he makes submissiveness his job, wagging his tail like a dog that wants to prove its loyalty to its masters.

43

Kaboura interpreted Saeed's submissive behavior by saying that sometimes even those with advanced degrees are cowards. All you have to do is wave your fist at them and they'll shit their pants. As if presenting irrefutable evidence of the correctness of his interpretation, Kaboura added, "If Saeed were a real man, or even just half a man, his wife never would have dared to betray him in front of his family with a boy who was still in his parents' care!" Kaboura may have been hurt by what was said about him, but I think that through his despicable, servile behavior Saeed wanted to prove to himself, and to the others in particular, that he was actually a kind, friendly, peaceable, hard-working, good-natured person, incapable of hurting even an ant, but that person who slit his wife's and daughter's throats from ear to ear without batting an eye may have had his soul possessed by an evil demon after drinking a bottle of whiskey on that sweltering summer night. It was clear that his guilt complex for what he had done continued to haunt and torture him. His terrifying screams while sleeping woke up all the prisoners on the cellblock. From time to time, he would burst out crying like a little boy orphaned early on in life. That is a precise description because I know all too well what it means for a little boy to become an orphan when the world is still unclear all around him.

But the time for talking about this matter hasn't arrived yet. . . .

What I would like to focus on is the fact that that Saeed's crime in and of itself wasn't important to Kaboura and the other prisoners. At the end of the day, they are no different than him. What I heard him say as I cleaned the toilets on a cold and dreary winter's day might be true, how there is no difference between someone who steals an egg and somebody who robs an entire bank, and how somebody who kills a single soul is the same as someone who commits a massacre in which the victims run into the scores, or even into the hundeds and thousands. In any event, behind bars, everyone is the same, and everyone finds himself naked before the truth of his actions. No matter how much you try to avoid it or make up stories or spin yourself into knots, you are in for a terrible disappointment. In the end, you don't reap anything but the others' laughter.

So, as I already mentioned, it wasn't Saeed's crime that piqued the curiosity of Kaboura and the other prisoners, but his wife. That's right, his beautiful wife. She was the fulcrum of their interests. They didn't talk about anything but her, not because she and her daughter had their throats slit from ear to ear, but because she was a hot, sexy woman, "as hot as an African pepper." With the passing of days, I realized how in a dismal prison with

44

blackish gray walls in every cell block, and on the cold concrete, behind high walls and iron bars, in the dim, foul-smelling cells, there is nothing but dreams of freeing oneself, and of hanging on to the relationship with the warmth of life on the outside, and with the absent, distant, female body. Ahhh. Look at me speaking like the philosophers and the poets, but I hope you won't find that strange of me. It's true that I dropped out of school but I was a sharp, active, and serious student. I was above average in every subject and outstanding in history and geography. That's right, I was outstanding in those two subjects. I still know a lot about Elissa who founded Carthage and the long wars of Hannibal against Rome and the conditions of Kairouan during the Aghlabid Era and the Spanish invasion of Tunisia and the nationalist leaders who resisted French colonialism. I'm very impressed with Asad Ibn al-Furat, who conquered Sicily, and Aziza Uthmana, "The Charitable, The Great, The Benefactress, The Honorable," as our history teacher used to call her, whose many good deeds included freeing slaves and circumcising poor children and orphans. This means that the Muslims had a virtuous woman before the Christians ever had Mother Teresa. I would have been a great friend to the leader Farhat Hached, and I know all about the Egyptian president Gamal Abdel Nasser and Mahatma Gandhi. I followed with great interest the case of the American president Bill Clinton and his flirtatious assistant. And when the Palestinians returned to Gaza I hung up a large picture of the leader Yasser Arafat in my bedroom.

As for those whom I hate, there are many. So many, in fact, that you would die of boredom if I rattled off all their names and nationalities for you.

Besides, you all must know how much I used to love reading. I read *Magdalene* by al-Manfaluti, *The Days* by Taha Hussein, *Midaq Alley* by Naguib Mahfouz, and *The Date and Its Clusters* by al-Bashir Khurayyif. Because I'm an enthusiast of history and geography, as I already mentioned, I read the greater part of *The Travels of Ibn Battuta*. I memorized some of Nizar Qabbani's poetry by heart as well as five poems by Abu al-Qasim al-Shabi, and the poem "Identity Card" by Mahmoud Darwish. I must mention how my eloquent voice and my superiority in history and geography attracted the attention of the bearded ones at one point, and they started to become friendly with me, expending everything in their power in order for me to become one of them. But Aziz, my friend from the south, warned me about them, saying, "It's better for you to put your hand inside a poisonous snake's pit than to become one of them yourself!" I think he was right about that.

That's right, I wasn't a bad or a lazy student, and I had once been intent upon continuing my studies until I received enough advanced degrees to allow me to take revenge on those who used to despise me in M Slum, but time had me in its sights. One day, all of my dreams were dashed, and I found myself running like a lunatic toward the gloomy destiny that awaited me.

Let me return to Saeed's wife, in order to say that nobody could stop talking about her. I'm certain that every prisoner used to sleep holding her body, imagining himself as that young man whom she chose as her lover, and who would fuck her until dawn, even as out there, far away, in the arid desert of the Persian Gulf, her duped husband loudly snored away. That's right, even if she were rotting bones, a woman could inflame the imagination of those deprived men behind the high walls and the metal bars. Isn't that right, my good people?

I don't deny that I was just like the others, longing for Saeed's wife to be mine. Before giving in to sleep, I would usually conjure up her image, which, due to the amount of talking and thinking about her, had become familiar to me, clear in my mind, as if I had known her for a long time. In the blink of an eye, my imagination ignites and cuts through the concrete walls and metal doors to transport me to a magical world. I can see myself on top of her in a big bed, like the beds of the princes of Baghdad during the age of Harun al-Rashid. She whispers beautiful words to me and I whisper more beautiful words back to her, and the world all around us is brilliant, suspended. Ahhhh . . . only dreams can make a person happy as he sleeps on cold concrete!

THE MOTHER

Please allow me to describe for you my condition when I reached six-teen years of age. Gloomy angst had sunk its claws into every part of my body. The world around me was all smoke and dust, cheerless mel-ancholy, as malicious, angry, and cruel eyes monitored my every move. I was in agony walking across the thorns of despair and frustration and impotence all night and all day. With the exception of Aunt Warda who maintained our friendship and mutual affection, everyone else turned against me, right down the line, and they remained doubtful about me, as if I was going to challenge them one day and cause a scandal in broad daylight. The harshest of all was my grandmother, who continued advising everyone to keep their eyes on me. I was imprisoned at home, only rarely going outside, and whenever I did so, I'd feel the entire vil-lage, its animals, vegetables, and minerals, monitoring me, scrutinizing every move I made, checking every word that fell from my tongue, so it wasn't be long before I hurried back into my room, depressed, to fall into long silent weeping.

What else could I do after getting kicked out of school for failing the elementary certificate exam twice in a row? What else could I do? I was past the age of maturity and on the verge of getting married. In our tiny dirt-poor village a young girl in a situation such as mine had no other choice but to consent to the way things are. If she tried to escape, to rebel against those stern rules, narrow-minded people would turn her into an ugly tale that they would talk about in private and in public.

By that point it would be likely for one of her male relatives to lose his head and shoot her or stab her, washing away the shame, defending the impugned honor, as people used to say in such circumstances. That's right, all of that was likely because the old embalmed heads still wanted to demonstrate their presence, in spite of the fact that they were all certain about leaving and never coming back, defying those many speeches we used to hear broadcast on the radio, gushing enthusiasm about women's freedom and women's rights. Blah, blah, blah. I won't hide from you that when I was that age I was untouched, fresh, like a flower that had started to open up, but living in permanent horror. That horror becomes even sharper and fiercer the more I thought about how, one day, one of those men I hated and who I'd sooner die than let his flesh touch mine was going to come and, amid the ululations and the songs, the beating of drums and the sounds of flutes, and the firing of the horsemen's rifles, bring me back to his house, close all the doors and take me as he got all puffed up like the winter wind and his family stood outside on the doorstep, ready to open fire in celebration of his masculinity's victory. That's right, this could happen, or something even worse could happen. I wouldn't be able to defend myself against the dangers threatening me as they accumulated on the horizon like deep-black clouds before a raging storm. That's right, I wouldn't be able to defend myself, isolated, all alone among my people. Not even Aunt Warda would be able to help me. She, too, would abandon me at the very last moment from fear of being persecuted by them, and of the injury they could bring upon her if she insisted on defending me and standing by my side. Not even my beauty would be able to save me. It's true that they say I'm the most beautiful woman in the village, but beauty for us is a liability, a danger to its possessor. In the end, victory is for the ugly and the unpleasant. I'm going to wilt away one day. My beauty will fade like that of many women who came before me. I'll be disfigured in body and soul, transformed into a woman whose only task is to have children and to serve her boorish husband behind closed doors. That's how I'm going to end up. Could God save me from that misfortune?

The sun rapidly passed toward the west. The shadows grew longer, covering the ravines and the lowlands. I could no longer see anything but small splotches of light upon the plain stretching out from our house toward the east, scattered here and there like pools of water left behind by last night's rains. Saliha repeats:

They drove your hamlet drove you and set out into the country / Where oh where have they taken you O pure beauty

Her mournful voice, seasoned with a distinctive raspiness that distinguished her from all other Tunisian singers, generated in me the desire to travel far, far away from our tiny dirt-poor village. A journey in which I would pass through the deserts and cross over the mountains to reach cities where I could protect myself from the harshness of starving Bedouin wolves. That's right, I wanted to go far, far away. There was no other salvation for me. Besides, those boys who I used to play hide-and-seek with on magnificent moonlit nights, with whom I used to steal figs and almonds and climb up to the peak of Mount Tirzah every fall, have moved on to Kairouan and other places after passing the elementary certificate examination. There they'll meet young ladies who might be more beautiful and more sweet-tongued than me. They'll forget about me altogether. That's right, they'll definitely forget all about me as I remain right here, withering and rotting away. I won't keep you waiting much longer, let me just say that I felt then like I was looking out over a darkened ravine and that in the blink of an eye someone was going to come and forcefully push me from behind into its depths.

THE SON

A little while back I told you about an American film. I mentioned how
affected I was by it, how attracted I was to its hero, that unemployed
young man who killed a lot of people in cold blood after running off with
his eccentric girlfriend, away from that small town where the two of them
used to live. I also mentioned how that film was powerfully present in
my mind when I perpetrated the monstrous act that brought me here to
death row. I used to love movies more than anything else. I had a particular taste for Westerns, violent films, and true crime. I saw a lot of movies
like that. You might even say I was addicted to watching them. I used to
identify with the heroes, especially those who got revenge for something
that had happened to them when they were younger or those who had
been deceived and double-crossed by people who once respected them
and treated them right. They were my favorite characters in the whole
world. That unemployed young man who could kill a man as easily as he'd
kill a fly was also one of my favorites, despite the fact that he doesn't
have the same characteristics I just laid out for you. But the one who was
truly closest to my heart was the hero of the film *Cool Hand Luke*, which
I had watched on French TV twice with my friend Aziz. Now this Luke
was a handsome young man, he didn't look anything like a criminal, but
he commits a series of shocking crimes and winds up sentenced to hard
labor in a terrible prison out in the middle of nowhere. From the start
Luke attracts the attention of the other prisoners with his defiant behavior and crafty smile, his irresistible attractiveness. He seems unaffected

by evil deeds in the world and by whatever physical or spiritual harm he may have personally caused. Even after he is viciously defeated in a boxing match he still manages to make his presence felt in that horrible place, filled with the most hardened criminals and killers, the most dishonest and unscrupulous people. Thanks to his intelligence, cleverness, and biting wit, as well as some tricks that demonstrate his cunning and shrewdness when the situation demands it, he earns the respect and friendship of the other prisoners. He even becomes close friends with the one who beat him so decisively in the boxing match. When the prison administration informs him of the death of his widowed mother with whom he was very close, despite her disapproval of his behavior, he refuses to cry in front of them and sadness only appears on his face for a brief moment. Instead, he picks up the guitar and in front of the other astonished prisoners he sings a song about hope and love. Ahh . . . I was so impressed! Outsmarting the heightened security and the barbed wire fence, Luke manages to escape from that terrible isolated prison. But after a violent pursuit with ferocious dogs they recapture him and throw him into a cell where he has to remain standing or nearly so for three weeks. Months later Luke tries to break out again but fails this time and is mercilessly beaten by the guards in plain sight of the other prisoners before being returned to the same cell. When he's finally released from there, they put painful chains on him, bind his legs, and force him to work all day in the same shameful position. But he doesn't break down, doesn't lose hope. He even comes up with some clever schemes to escape those harsh conditions. There he is showing loyalty and blind obedience to the prison guards. There he is degrading himself before them, wagging his tail like an obedient dog, impervious to the contempt that many of the other prisoners have started to show him because of his submissive behavior. Until one day, Luke and his friend who defeated him in the boxing match escape in a prison truck right under the noses of their heavily armed captors. The pursuit begins all over again and the barking of ferocious dogs rings out loudly in those empty spaces. One night the security forces surround the two escaped prisoners and demand they give themselves up. Certain that escape from the siege imposed all around them is impossible, the guy who defeated him at boxing tries to convince Luke to comply with the orders of the security forces immediately and unconditionally, but Luke leaves him behind and runs off to find himself inside an abandoned church. At that moment, he raises his head toward the sky and begins speaking to God, asking Him why he deserves this gloomy destiny. He's still talking to God, who remains silent in the heavens above, when the security forces surround the church, demanding through their bullhorns that he give himself up. But he doesn't. As he edges closer to the window and tries to see what's going on outside, a sniper's bullet slams into him, and he's carried off to the hospital with that crafty smile he had become famous for among the prisoners still on his lips. Upon returning to the prison, Luke's friend tells his comrades all about Luke's final adventure that cost him his life, pausing for a long time on his cunning smile that lit up his handsome face as the ambulance rushed him to the hospital. At the end he shouts, inspired, "Old Luke, he was some boy. Cool Hand Luke. Hell! He's a natural-born world-shaker."

I won't hide the fact that I was very impressed with that last sentence, "He's a natural-born world-shaker." After I saw the film I started repeating it in front of Aziz as if it were my favorite song, hoping he would like it as much as I did, but he remained silent and apathetic. After I stared at him, he turned red with anger and shouted at me, "Listen, Alaa al-Din, movies aren't real life and life isn't a movie. You've got to keep your feet on the ground or you're never going to succeed. Never!"

Of course his words didn't bring me any comfort. They seemed silly and meaningless because I had always believed and still do believe that life is a movie and that movies imitate life—the scumbags, murderers, hypocrites, charlatans, the immoral, vagabonds, pimps, tricksters, slanderers, but also the gentle, noble, the good-hearted, those who are truthful in speech and in action, as well as those who we see in the movies are all, in my opinion, exactly like the people we meet in real life. Besides, I also believe that Cool Hand Luke really did want to change the world, whereas the others—and they are the overwhelming majority of humanity—are willing to go along with the status quo, even if that clashes with their attitudes and instincts, their feelings and their sentiments. He was always trying to establish himself outside the laws that people with influence and power determine and decide. In short, he was like a bird that always wants to sing a different song than the rest of the flock. That's exactly what Aziz, who hasn't visited me once since I set foot in this prison, is unable to understand. I never saw his face in court either. In the one terse letter he sent me about two months after my arrest, he told me that my memory hadn't betrayed me and that it was my attraction to violence and crime films that made me lose my life.

Me, lose my life! I have something to say about that expression. I'd like to say to my friend Aziz, whether or not he ever hears this, that ever since the age of seventeen I realized that my life was going to be a series of consecutive losses, so I decided to end it with that monstrous act. After all, what's the point of a human being living a long life marked by consecutive losses, one after another? That's what Cool Hand Luke realized, too. He didn't hesitate to stick his neck out to be hit by that fatal bullet because he could no longer bear to live a life in which losses were followed by humiliations, like successively repeating telegraph poles in the arid desert. I won't deny the fact that Cool Hand Luke had been with me before I ever committed my crime, and he was with me the day I carried it out. He was my friend and my brother in prison throughout the period leading up to my trial, and he's here with me now in this cell on death row. I believe he's going to escort me to the gallows one cold, silent, sad dawn, and I'll go up to the gallows with a crafty smile on my lips like the one that was lighting up his face as he was taken away in the ambulance after that fatal bullet.

THE MOTHER

Please allow me to take you to another chapter of my life. As I have assured you from the start, I'm going to tell you everything with the utmost sincerity and honesty and clarity, because I'm now in a world where I no longer have any need for symbolism or secrecy or dissimulation. I must point out that I didn't mean to make fun of them or mess with their minds as they thought I did when I responded to that question they asked me on that blazing-hot morning in the early summer of 1978. But why else would they have stared at me in astonishment like that, as amazed as if I had uttered some riddled speech that harbored within it a feminine trap that would be hard for them to get out of or avoid its snares? That's right, that's what happened to them as soon as I uttered my clear and honest response. Afterward they were silent and frozen in front of me until they came to resemble stones from the time of Noah. Then they dispersed all around me, silent, astonished, perplexed. When they came back asking me the very same question, I gave them the same response. This happened again and again, and every time I would respond with the same answer to the same question. Nevertheless, they wouldn't budge. They grew more and more doubtful and suspicious of me. They would consult each other in private, perhaps in order to discover the trap they thought I had laid for them. When they were done, they would return to ask me the very same question, and they wouldn't hear anything from me except for the same answer, whether that was in the morning or the evening, in the light of day or the darkness of night. So that you can all be clear on this matter, let me tell you the facts of what happened on that blazing-hot morning in the early summer of that year. . . .

I had just woken up, and it was already mid-morning when they entered my room and surrounded me on all sides, as if they were afraid I might fly out the window. They all took a long hard look at me. My grand-mother had wrapped her head in a black scarf that she would always wear whenever the chronic migraines that she suffered from in her old age flared up. Deep wrinkles appeared on her sallow face, and in a trembling voice she asked me, "Do you know Mansour?"

I dug through my memory a little bit, and then replied, "Yes."

They exchanged glances as beads of sweat glistened on their faces. Then, inclining her head toward me, my grandmother said, "Yesterday Mansour came to see your father. He said he wants to get engaged. What do you think?"

Without any hesitation, I replied, "I don't have any objections!"

That's when what I told you about a little while ago happened. In the end they sent Aunt Warda, who had been visiting her daughter in Kairouan, to hear "the last word" from me. Aunt Warda came to see me in the evening. The crescent moon was adorning the star-studded sky as though it were a silver necklace and the universe was brilliant, that awe-inspiring tranquillity and summery magnificence wrapped up in soft, gentle darkness, in which purple blended into silver, straining to continue on until infinity. After we greeted each other and embraced, Aunt Warda told me about Fatiha, her oldest daughter who had gotten married two years before, about the markets of Kairouan where she got lost more than once, and about the long hours she had spent at the Sidi al-Suhbi shrine praying for my blessings and well being and happiness. So that God would answer her prayers, she lit candles at the shrine of the pious saint. Then she turned to the heart of the matter, asking me if I was serious about Mansour, and I told her the same thing I had repeatedly told the others. She was also struck with astonishment. Her mouth hung open for several minutes. She didn't know what to say or do. Then she took my right hand and her frankincense-perfumed breath tickled my face as she told me in her tender warm voice, "My little girl, tell me the truth, don't hide a single thing from me!"

"Auntie, on the head of Sidi al-Suhbi, what I've told you is the truth."

"Meaning, you're happy with him?"

"Happy with him today and tomorrow and forever after!"

Aunt Warda's face relaxed. She kept silent for a bit, and then, with tears shimmering in her eyes like little stars, said, "My little girl, may God please you and grant you good fortune. May God, who has delighted me, also delight your heart!"

Then she stood up. When she reached the door she let out an ululation and its echo broke apart in the summer night like sparkling silver.

The truth of the matter is that it was natural that my accepting Mansour as a husband would elicit the amazement and confusion of my family. I didn't know anything about him besides what I had heard from other people. People used to say he had left the village when he was seventeen, after losing both of his parents in the same year, and traveled to the capital without even enough money to last one week. It turns out that he lived for the first three years in misery and hunger, but that he later found work on the railroad. His circumstances improved. The proof is that he built a house for himself in the capital, where he had once arrived poor and destitute. He had disappeared from the village for years and years, to the point that his family nearly forgot about him. But then he started to visit them regularly, taking care to show up for harvests and holidays as well as for wedding parties and funeral processions. Everyone who got close to him insisted that his pockets were full and that the wound of his painful past had healed completely. He no longer talked to people as if he were beneath them, like he used to do. Instead, he started treating them, even the notables, as equals. Because he was a boy made good from that dirt-poor village, making a name for himself in that big, rough capital city, everyone started to show him esteem and respect. I heard that during those regular visits that brought him to the village Mansour took care to tell some of his relatives how he wanted to marry a girl from his "blood," and from the same soil that had witnessed his birth, because the girls of the capital, in his opinion, were "corrupt and lewd and unworthy of the world or religion." Because this would guarantee the protection of blood ties for him and for them, the idea pleased his relatives very much. And so they started searching high and low for the young lady who would be suitable for this village boy who had become a respectable and well-off man. After knocking on a lot of doors, they called off their search when it became clear to them that all of the pretty girls and "the girls of origin," as they are called in our village, were exhibiting subtle opposition to marrying him. This wasn't surprising. Mansour wasn't the kind of man who turned women's heads or stirred up their hidden desires. He was ugly, frail, and limped slightly because of an illness it is said he contracted in early childhood. He was extremely shy, especially around women. In short, Mansour was one of those ordinary men who leave no trace behind in the memory of the people he meets, not even with those he has sat with for an hour or two or even more. He looked like a sad gray bird that can't sing and doesn't chirp, one that wouldn't make a sound, but instead just looks down at people during times of dryness and drought, only to suddenly disappear into the dust and yellow smoke. Certain that the mere mention of Mansour's name would send me running for the hills, Mansour's relatives didn't even bother to come near our front door. At that time, I was notorious throughout the village and even in neighboring villages for being an obstinate young woman. Anyone who dared to approach me and ask for my hand would come up against impossible demands that would send him running away as quickly as possible, head over heels. But Mansour came in the beginning of that blazing-hot summer, dressed in a smart white suit that made him slightly less ugly, and in complete calm and simplicity he approached my father as he sat drinking mint tea in front of the shop of his mellow friend the parfumier, and greeted him with respect and warmth. After telling him about the capital and its state of affairs, about its turmoil and its problems that have no beginning or end, he asked him with absolute grace and manners, without stuttering as he usually did whenever he approached a complicated and thorny issue, if he could present himself to ask for the hand of his daughter, Najma. For a few minutes, my father bowed his head, without moving, because what he just heard was something he never would have expected. Maybe during those few minutes he remembered how he had been when he first heard that my mother wanted to marry him. Then he raised his head and stared into the face of that frail young man sitting there in front of him, trying to discern the secret of this new-found courage. After making sure that the one sitting before him was no longer that orphaned and defeated youngster he once was, and had become instead a well-adjusted and self-assured man, he patted him on the shoulder with the tenderness of an affectionate, merciful father, and said, "Give me some time before I respond to your request, my son!" Then he said goodbye and walked home, one step forward, two steps back, because he was afraid of how angry my mother would be when he told her what had happened. After lunch he was no longer able to hide it from her, and he laid it all out, his voice trembling, his saliva all dried up. Contrary to what he had expected, though, my mother

57

was happy about the situation and welcomed it, she was even enthusiastic. In a clear tone of joyfulness, she said, "This is something that delights the heart, my daughter has grown up and needs to get married today, not tomorrow!" Then she rushed over to see my grandmother and asked for her help. After listening with extreme interest, my grandmother shoved some black tobacco into her cheeks, and in a resolute voice affirmed that she would do the impossible so that I would consent, so that I would marry Mansour. Maybe she imagined I was standing at her door eavesdropping on what she was saying, because at that moment she shouted, "What's wrong with Mansour? He's a man's man, he's got morals and modesty and a house in the capital. What more could she want? Or would she rather sit night and day with the door to her heart shut tight, until she becomes unmarriageable and winds up a stinking corpse who all the men would run away from before touching. What does she want, I wonder? Tell me, what does she want?"

The next morning my grandmother led the caravan that came to inform me what was happening.

I know you all are going to accuse me of various things, that you're going to call me the ugliest of names, that you're going to say I'm a liar, a hypocrite, trash, without a conscience. Otherwise how could I have consented to marry a man I didn't love, that is, someone who I didn't have any emotional connection with? I know all of this. But seeing as how I promised you from the start that I would be honest, I tell you that I consented to marry Mansour without any hesitation or fear, fleeing from that horrible image that had been pursuing me day and night. The image of that darkened ravine. I'm looking down into it, someone's going to come in the blink of an eye and toss me into its depths. That's the honest truth. Besides, my life in that dirt-poor village had truly become an intolerable hell. So my goal was to get out of there as soon as possible, regardless of the price I'd have to pay, or the means I'd have to use. Doesn't someone who is lost in the desert hope for a drop of water to avoid death by thirst? That was my condition at the time. So I consented to marry Mansour. I must confess to you that the awful hole left behind by those I had shared the joys of childhood with made me yearn to be with them again, because staying behind in the village was going to lead me either to madness or death, so I grabbed onto the first lifeline I was thrown as I was on the verge of falling into that darkened ravine. That lifeline was Mansour.

THE SON

You can ask me about the person or about the people whom I'd like to meet and speak with during these last weeks, or these last days of my life. It's within your rights because it's natural to ask such a question of someone like me, whose departure from this world is imminent. Let me begin with those who aren't kin or relatives. I'll be straight with you and say that the only person who I really want to sit with out of all of them is my friend Aziz; rather, let me say, my brother Aziz, because he was like a brother to me. He was affectionate with me and merciful toward me, helping me out when times were tough, comforting me when my wounds bled, and standing by my side when I was at my wit's end and my horizons turned to black. It's true that he didn't visit me in prison, not even once, and he didn't write me anything more than one dry letter that was all blame and reproof and reprimand. Neither did he show up for any of my court hearings. Be that as it may, how much I would like to sit with him, if only for an hour, to tell him everything that's in my heart, and to thank him profusely for all the good he has done for me through all the lean years I spent before committing my monstrous act. Ahh . . . how much I would like that! I remember clearly the first time we met. At the time, I had dropped out of school and started wandering the streets in search of work that would cover my room and board, because I had started to think about leaving home once and for all. Besides, living in that filthy slum had become unbearable. I was willing to accept any kind of work at all, including washing dishes or sweeping the streets. At first I worked as

59

a waiter in a popular restaurant in Bab Suwayqa, but the owner fired me after ten days without giving me a reason why, and so it was that I went back to canvassing the streets from morning until night, only returning home, with swollen feet of course, after having made certain that the people of the slum had already gone to sleep since I could no longer put up with their whisperings and slanderous gossip, their derisive laughter, and the indecent words they used to hurl at me whenever I passed by them. I won't hide the fact that I started to be afraid, to lose my self-confidence, and to regret dropping out of school. From time to time, crying fits would overcome me, sometimes even when I was walking through the streets and around other people. My circumstances continued to deteriorate day after day until I started to think about throwing myself under the train arriving from Bizerte that passed through the slum at dawn. This black thought proceeded to grow and grow until it started to fill the world all around me. My mind was preoccupied with it when someone asked if they could sit down next to me in that small café in Bab al-Khadra, and I assented without even looking up at him. He lit a cigarette and ordered an espresso. Almost ten minutes passed without my looking at him, while I tried to imagine the opinions and feelings of everyone I knew, whether they were relatives or non-relatives, when they were informed that I had been transformed into scraps of flesh and bone beneath the train arriving from Bizerte on one mournful dawn rising with the colors of the face of a drowned man whose corpse continued to decompose in the water for days on end. Then I heard the man sitting beside me ask if I wanted a cigarette. It was only in this moment that I looked up at him. The smile on his face allowed him to enter my heart immediately. A smile that seemed as though it had been on his face since birth, and remained radiant on his face even after he reached the age of twenty. Maybe it won't even leave him once he becomes an old man, inching along like an ant. It's the smile of those creatures who achieve happiness for themselves through conviction and satisfaction with whatever utterly simple things life sends their way. It's enough, for example, for someone like that to wake up in the morning to the sweet voice of Fairuz as she sings about the beauty of the sweet girl preparing the morning bread, in order to spend the entire day flying through the air, joyful and delighted. It seemed to me that the thin, olive-skinned young man sitting beside me was one of those angelic creatures—likeable, guilelesss, his soul empty of wickedness and meanness and cunning and evil. So I took to him and accepted the cigarette, I who

60

had never known the taste of cigarettes until that very moment. As if he had known me for a long time, the young man started telling me all about himself and his life, relaxed and easygoing, and I grew increasingly comfortable around him. From what he said I learned that he was from a small village near Medenine and that he had come to the capital when he was eighteen years old (the same age as me at the time) to work with his uncle in a used clothing store in the Hafsia neighborhood. I also learned that he lived alone in a "studio" in the same neighborhood, and that things were going pretty well for him, because his uncle was a kind man, who loved him and showed him great affection, thinking a lot about his future. He loved his uncle as well, respecting and exalting him, and thought he was the greatest human being alive, maybe even better than his father. He quickly corrected himself and said, "No, no. The comparison between my uncle and my father isn't correct because each one of them has his special place in my heart. But in my opinion my uncle is better than all my other maternal and paternal uncles. He understands me in the blink of an eye and I understand him. Until my dying breath I won't ever forget the kindnesses he's shown me. He saved me from unemployment when I dropped out of school. He got me out of that tiny miserable village where I used to live and brought me to the capital, which I quickly came to know as well as I know my own pocket. He let me do whatever I wanted after getting off work. He didn't monitor me or restrict my movements. He didn't get angry with me except when there was good reason to do so. For sure I'm very lucky to have an uncle like him." He added how at first he had stayed with his uncle in his house in the Ibn Khaldun neighborhood, but after a year he wanted to become more independent. It was his uncle who in less than twenty-four hours found him a clean and cheap studio apartment near the store where he worked. The thin young man told me all of this information in one dose, without doubting my intentions at all, and without asking a single question to get to know me better. Maybe that was why I plunged headlong into conversation so enthusiastically, as if I was close to that young man sitting beside me in that small café in Bab al-Khadra; it wasn't as cold and dark there as it had been when I was sitting there all by myself, sinking in my black concerns, thinking about what kind of responses there would be from family and friends if news reached them one morning about my suicide beneath the wheels of the train rolling in from Bizerte: it would be melancholy, just like any time such misfortunes and tragedies take place. As the thin, olive-skinned young man was telling me all about his life and difficult circumstances, without beating around the bush at all, I found myself tripping over my words because I was forced to hide some related truths, especially those concerning my relationship with my mother, but other things as well. Among what I said was how my father had left his village, located eighty kilometers west of Kairouan, when he was seventeen years old. Upon reaching the age of twenty, he found work on the railroad.

My father was twenty-seven when he married my mother, who was from the same village. I was ten years old when he got sick with an incurable disease and died within a few short days. His death was the first and most shocking tragedy I ever faced. Afterward I felt that life had become empty and meaningless. That is one hundred percent true. As for my mother, I said that she is a harsh, heartless woman. In contrast to my father, she only rarely took any interest in me, and she always treated me as if I wasn't her son. Ever since my early childhood she quarreled with me all the time and insulted me with the nastiest names—I'm a dung beetle and a sewer rat and the offspring of mangy mutts, and on and on and on. Because of her harshness toward me I found myself forced to leave school, in spite of the fact that I was an outstanding student, especially in history and geography. Around that time she started asking me with extreme insistence to go look for work, threatening to kick me out of the house if I didn't. That isn't exactly true, but I wanted to create a distorted image of her, and it appeared that I had succeeded in doing so because distaste and disgust at that heartless and mean-spirited creature appeared clearly on the young man's face. When I started telling him about my grandmother, tears scorched my eyes. In a quavering voice, I said that my grandmother was, as far as I was concerned, the dearest creature in the whole world after my father. Rather, she might have had the very same status he had in my heart. I was overjoyed whenever I went to visit her in the village, which my mother always described as "dirt poor." At first, I would go with my father, but after his death I began to visit her alone, when I had the day off, and also on holidays and harvests. Every time I visited her, she received me with tears in her eyes. That was also how she would be when she said goodbye to me. She used to tell me wondrous tales at night. I continued listening to her tell those stories until I grew up. During the day, especially when the weather was nice, she would take me on walks through the olive and almond groves. That used to please me very much and make me forget all about my mother's harshness and loathing, as well as the degeneracy of the people of the slum we lived in, those who I didn't like and those who didn't like me.

At this point I broke down crying, and I stopped talking as I heaved. Just then, the young man patted me on the shoulder gently and tenderly and said, "Don't worry, God always provides!"

Then, after a moment of silence, he asked me, "Do you really want to find work?"

"Yes, I do. As soon as possible."

He thought for a bit, and then said, "Listen, the best thing I can do for you right now is introduce you to my uncle. He's on good terms with the owner of a café near the central market. I'm sure he'll help you get work there as a waiter."

"That's very good to hear!"

The young man squeezed my hand forcefully and said, "My name's Aziz. Glad to meet you!"

From that small café in Bab al-Khadra we immediately headed for the used clothing store in Hafsia, where Aziz's uncle welcomed us warmly. He was a very dark-skinned man, bald, short, with gaps between his teeth and a big paunch that he loved to stroke with his right hand from time to time. He was sporting a track suit and tennis shoes. After Aziz explained my situation to him, his uncle Miftah studied me carefully for a long time, then said, "Come back to see me tomorrow, in the afternoon. Inshallah there'll be something."

I went back to see him the next afternoon, and he gave me the address and name of the café and told me, "My friend's waiting for you over there. Go see him right away."

I walked over there, and the very next day I started working at al-Salam Café.

At that time, the winter that had outworn its welcome for the year was starting to rapidly come to an end. As the warmth heralding spring crept gently and calmly into my veins, I sensed the winter that had been wrapped around my soul also starting to die. An amazing light beamed out of its frigid darkness and started to wash over me, when all of a sudden I realized for the first time how life is the most beautiful gift that God bestows upon humanity, so one must live its length and breadth and not fritter away a single moment in order to deserve it at all. And so it was that the spring that had sprung inside my soul embraced the spring that had started to wash over the world, restraining my bitter feelings of orphanhood and loneliness, which had persisted in tormenting me and interrupting my sleep for many years. It's certain that Aziz was the one with the magic wand causing those awesome transformations that unexpectedly took place in my life.

I must confess that I could no longer bear being apart from him, and that I started to be influenced by his ideas and his rosy outlook on life, an outlook that said you must live for today and cast tomorrow to the fates to do with you whatever they wish and however they please. His outlook also predicates that we deserve to live far removed from everything that can ruin life and make it miserable. Because his advice proved its worth and benefit, I started implementing it with complete devotion, as well as exerting all of my energy to beam from my face that southern, sunny disposition that marked his personality. Every day, I would make a point of seeing him. It delighted me to accompany him to the cafés of Bab al-Bahr and the cinema halls and the northern suburbs when time, wallet, and weather permitted. Usually I would spend the night with him in the clean studio where he lived, not far from where he worked. With him, I learned how to chat up girls, to drink beer, and how to do many other things. In short, I can say that the happiest times of my life were those I spent in the company of Aziz, and that my most inspiring adventures were those that I lived with him. Under the influence of my daily interaction with him, my nature softened, my mood relaxed, my volcanoes calmed down, and I was no longer as quick to anger or to cry, or to become anxious as I had been before. By and by, I stopped paying much mind to the people of the slum. I would tell myself as I was coming home or leaving the house that I had to forget about them, to shut my ears against their fabricated stories, against their indecent words and slanderous rumors. I behaved as though they weren't even present at all, and I'd tell myself I had to hold my head up high, to defy them, and to stare back at them as if they were repulsive insects that didn't even deserve to be crushed underfoot. Yeah, that's what I would tell myself as I made my way to work at the café early in the morning, or came home from there at the end of the night. My behavior around my mother changed as well. The temper tantrums that once consumed me whenever I found myself face to face with her, or whenever she wanted to give me some advice as I was heading to bed or just opening my eyes from sleep, heavy with terrible nightmares, or whenever she talked to me about something concerning me or concerning her, had all ended. It's true, that was how I used to behave around her before I met

Aziz. I used to scream in her face at the top of my lungs. I would break dishes, hurling kitchen or bathroom supplies up in the air. These temper tantrums of mine grew more intense after my father's death, to the point that they even started happening more than once in the same day. At first, my mother would scream right back in my face, threatening me with this or that punishment, but, with the passing of time, she chose to confront me with silence and patience and disinterest—weapons of those who have mastered life well and who have tasted both its bitterness and its sweetness. But after I got to know Aziz, I no longer did those sorts of things around her—I no longer raised my voice, I no longer broke dishes, and I no longer stirred up a tempest in a teacup; rather, I started to come home calmly and leave calmly. Sometimes I would address myself with a rebuke after turning away from her, saying, "Shame on you. Shame on you. You're mistreating your own mother. In the future you'll have to not pay much heed to the rumors and fabricated lies that the scumbags of the slum say about her. Shame on it all. Shame on you!" At the café, my psychological and professional circumstances were as good as could be hoped for, and the owner, Hajj Marzouq, who was from a village in the south not far from Aziz's village, respected me and held me in high regard. From time to time he would praise my nimbleness and my elegant speech, especially with the respectable customers, something that used to stir up the envy and jealousy of the other waiters, including those who had spent more than half their life working in cafés.

But one day, with autumn on the way, as the capital started to reclaim its vitality and its frenetic pace that follows the indolence of summer and accompanies the end of vacation and the return to school, I saw one of those pests from the slum sitting at the counter, sipping his coffee, a cigarette hanging from the left corner of his lips, filthy from so much smoking. He watched me scornfully, the features on his face indicating he was extremely happy and delighted to have discovered where I worked, as though he were a hunter who had only after great difficulty found the prey that had once escaped him, certain that it wasn't about to succeed in escaping a second time. At that moment, I got all confused; I got so mixed up that I was no longer able to control myself. Just then, the tray I had been carrying with three cups of tea, four cups of coffee, a bottle of spring water, and one of Coca-Cola fell to the ground. The racket made by all that clattering to the ground made the customers lift their heads and fix their eyes upon me and I was as embarrassed as if I had farted in front of them. The café owner didn't get as upset as he would have with the other waiters when they made the same kinds of mistakes. Instead, he sufficed by saying, in a tone with a bit of loathing and beratement, "Watch it, Alaa al-Din. I hope nothing like this ever happens again." In the blink of an eye, I saw that son of a bitch, his face dripping with all the filth of the world, looking at me accusingly. This time his expression showed how much he wanted to humiliate me and tell the café owner and the customers, in a loud voice, all of the fabricated rumors that he and the other scumbags of the slum like him used to spread about my mother. Let me just say that if I had the necessary physical powers, I would have attacked him right then and there and taught him a lesson he would never forget until Azrael quelled his breaths. But what does a little lamb do in the face of a fearsome wolf? That's how I was with that son of a bitch who continued staring at me accusingly, scornfully, my hands shaking as I picked up all the shards of glass and the scattered fragments of cups, my shoes and clothes splattered with tea and coffee, and all eyes fixed on me, as autumn swept up the first leaves that had fallen onto the ground in front of the café. When that son of a bitch walked out after almost twenty minutes had passed since the tray dropped, the spring that was in my heart had sprung once again, and I prayed to God more than once, beseeching Him to let me see that bastard in the café just one more time.

After getting off work at six, I ran to Hafsia, searching at Aziz's for something that could ease my mind. When he suggested I go with him to Tabarka, I forgot all about that son of a bitch from the café. The next morning, I asked Hajj Marzouq for three days off and he gave them to me without any hesitation. And so it was that Aziz and I went to Tabarka. When we got back to the capital, while I was still reminiscing about the enchanting natural scenery I had seen on my holiday, especially at sunrise and sunset, I felt that the time had come for me to discover the world, and that the day when I would leave that filthy slum was imminent. But after just three days back at work, that son of a bitch showed up again, this time with three of his pals, and standing there in the middle of them was the mortal enemy of my departed father and my mother and, of course, of me too. After ordering four cups of coffee and a bottle of spring water, they fixed their eyes upon me and started to watch everything I did. From time to time, they leaned in close to one other, and continued whispering for several minutes, until they burst out laughing. What I had feared as soon as they came into the café came to pass. The tray dropped out of my hand again and I found myself in a much worse situation than the last time. This time, the blood rose to Hajj Marzouq's head, and he berated me in a loud voice, so loud that I almost broke out crying from the intensity of my humiliation. That's right, this is the state I was in as they whispered to each other and guffawed scornfully, as if I were a monkey in the circus. They were proud to have that son of a bitch everyone in the slum was so afraid of with them. He had a thick voice and dilated eyes that were perpetually red, a flattened head, a face swollen with fat and flesh disfigured by old knife wounds, a mouth as large as that of an aged crocodile, a neck like a castrated bull, and he wore enormous variously shaped rings on the fingers of his left hand. He was pleased to be the aggrandized boss of an evil gang that spreads corruption and cruelty throughout the slum, violates the people's honor, and violently assaults in the light of day those who had no strength and no power. In those bitter moments, I no longer saw anything in front of me except what that repulsive man had done to my late father on that distant day, when I was nine years old, that terrible day that might be the main reason why he was afflicted with the awful illness that took his life within the span of a few short days. I must explain to all of you what happened. Over the course of many months, that bastard kept following my mother around, harassing her, and doing everything in his power to make her fall for him. When his efforts came to nothing, he began to threaten her and vow revenge, forcing her to listen to vulgarities whenever she was coming home or leaving the house. When she couldn't take it any longer, she complained to my father. To be completely honest with you, I must say that my father was extremely panicked when he heard this. I saw him crumple up like a mouse that suddenly finds itself facing a cat that has chased it and made its life miserable for days on end. That didn't surprise me. God had protected my father with His vast grace, a peaceable man who took care to steer clear of the evil of others, and who liked to live far removed from anything that could disturb his life or cause him any harm, however small or large. Besides, he was one of those people who chose to spend their days following a single routine: home to work and work to home, so he wouldn't sit around for very long in cafés, he didn't mix with the people of the slum, and he only made conversation with them on rare occasions. His sole pleasure was to sit in front of the television for long hours and follow world news or to watch Egyptian and other serials, so it was perfectly natural for him to be hit with panic when my mother told him about what that son of a bitch, feared by everyone in the neighborhood because of his typically unjustified aggressiveness and his perpetual tendency to get into fights and pick on the weak, was doing to her. For a few long minutes, he remained silent, pale-faced, not saying anything and not doing anything, his back hunched over slightly as if he was about to receive a whipping from behind. At that point, my mother grumbled angrily, "If you knew from the start that you'd be incapable of protecting me from the beasts of this slum, why'd you marry me in the first place?" My father didn't comment on the deadly insult my mother flung at him, but instead grew more panicked and crumpled, to the point that she sensed that in those moments he wished he had never been born. As my mother prepared to go to sleep earlier than usual, she said to him, "I'm sure you'll slip out the window naked and barefoot when that son of a bitch assaults me one day while I'm with you in the bedroom." His face turned red, then yellow, then green, but he didn't utter a single word; rather, he mumbled a little bit, and then fell silent. As for me, I went to bed with the sense that the next day was going to be one in which the victims were going to be forced to march barefoot across the thorns of humiliation and shame.

And that's what actually happened.

The filthy drizzle of autumn fell on the slum, drowning in mud and clay, enshrouded by the dreariness of Sunday morning. Without drinking his coffee, my father plunged out into the street, on his face the grim determination of someone who wants to wash away a shame that has sullied his personal honor and the honor of his family, even if it cost him his life. Running after him, my little body shivered in the bitter morning cold, and my heart thumped violently even as he imperiously ordered me to return home at once. I obeyed him. I stood by the door, straining to see what was about to happen. When he reached the house of that son of a bitch, which was approximately two hundred meters from ours, my father started pounding on the metal door with loud consecutive blows, and the evil son of a bitch suddenly peeked out his flattened head, his frowning face, and his ever-red dilated eyes. My father shouted so loudly at him that I imagined whoever had made that shout couldn't possibly have been my father, but had to have been someone else I had never met before. I heard him say in a tone of incredible defiance, "Listen up, if you ever dare harass my wife again, I'll teach you a lesson nobody in this slum ever has!" Without grunting even a single syllable, that bastard stopped him with a powerful punch that brought my father down to the ground and filled his mouth with blood. When he tried to get up, he beat him back down to the ground again with a violent kick, and then started kicking him some more, stomping his shoes on his face and his chest and his stomach, as his visage became swollen in fury and rage. From time to time, he bent down and grabbed my father by the collar, then stood him up on his feet and landed a punch or two or even more, and then threw him to the ground, as though he were a bug that didn't deserve to exist. My father received those blows and punches and kicks with the silence and submissiveness of someone who has no power and no strength in the face of a beast of prey to whom he had just offered a golden opportunity to show off its strength and might. The people of the slum watched it all happen, the big and the small, women and men alike, and many of them hoped that the punches and the kicks and the insults would last forever, and that it would break up the dreariness of a routine Sunday morning in that miserable filthy slum for all its migrants and swindlers and pickpockets and pimps and drug dealers. I watched it all from behind the mist of my profusely falling tears. I have no idea what my mother thought as she watched my father rolling around in the autumn mud amid the dreariness of Sunday morning.

Those horrifying images from the past cycled through my mind one after another as I stood there amid the shattered fragments of cups, porcelain pieces strewn all over the place, as my boss Marzouq shouted at me scoldingly, and those depraved men watched me scornfully, accusingly, flanking my father's murderer. That's right, I say my father's murderer because that's what he really is, even if he didn't do it directly. After that black Sunday, my father's circumstances started to deteriorate continuously, especially on the moral and psychological levels. Gray conquered his hair. His back grew more and more hunched. In the features of his sallow face, wrinkles appeared clear and well defined; at home he no longer watched television the way he used to, and he became apathetic about what was going on in the world. Even the events in Iraq and Palestine that he used to follow with great interest ceased to interest him. Nothing interested him anymore, not even the natural disasters whose victims rose into the scores or even the hundreds. He was distracted all the time and he could barely stay focused on people or objects. He no longer treated me, his only son, kindly, and he no longer looked at me except out of the corner of his eye. I think that he didn't see anything anymore except for that dreadful image, the image of himself being thrown into the mud, his face and his clothes stained with blood, on his chest the heavy boots of that son of a bitch, who was all puffed up with pride, brilliant from the glorious victory he had achieved. As for his relationship with my mother, which had always been poor, the last of its threads were cut after that painful incident, and their presence together under the same roof became as though it had been imposed by an invisible force that neither one recognized.

One dusty gloomy night, my father breathed his last breath in the Charles-Nicole Hospital in the capital. My mother didn't shed a single tear of sorrow for him and didn't pay me any attention after those scumbags left. Wolves always return to where they know they will prevail over innocent and lost sheep. They really did come back two days later. Then they started showing up at the al-Salam Café every day, as if it were the only café in the entire capital. Sometimes they would show up in the morning and in the evening. They would always stare at me with contempt and schadenfreude, letting me know through their movements and gestures that I wasn't going to get away from them, and that they were going to humiliate me one day in front of all of the customers at the café. When they started talking to Hajj Marzouq, exchanging jokes and stories with him, chortling loudly, I realized that the time for implementing their hellish plan against me was imminent, so I played sick and took five days off.

The truth of the matter is that I had decided to finally quit working there. You might question my decision and ask me, "But why did you rush off and make that decision if you knew that what those scumbags were going to say to Hajj Marzouq or to any customer in the café would be nothing but the same lies they had spread throughout the slum, and that it wouldn't be too hard for you to refute one after another?" I'd say to you: You are mistaken right down the line, my friends. Reality in our country affirms with incontrovertible evidence that people tend to believe rumors, even when they know they are rumors; otherwise, how else would you make sense of their rapid spread, which resembles fire spreading through dry kindling, achieved by lies and gossip, whereas the truth can remain mute for a long time, unknown? When it is finally exposed, the time for it to be as beneficial and useful as it needs to be has already passed. In my short life I have seen many liars and charlatans standing up proud and pleased with themselves even as the masses call for their heads to roll. As for the truthful in speech and action, I have seen some of them withdraw defeated, humiliated, or sitting among the people who despise them, their heads bowed, hung like all those who have committed unforgivable sins. There's nothing amazing therefore about Hajj Marzouq believing those scumbags' lies, and running off incensed and all worked up to inform Aziz's uncle of the incredible things he has heard. The latter claps his hands together in regret, and says, "Forgive me, brother Marzouq, by God I didn't mean to deceive you. Why would I do that after all these years we've shared water and salt? But in this greedy time, a person is no longer capable of distinguishing between the good and the bad. I saw the good in that young man when he showed up with my nephew asking for help and assistance, and I immediately sent him to you without knowing that his family is offensive and incompatible with morals and religion!" Then Aziz's uncle goes to see his nephew. After guiding him into an out-of-the-way corner he makes him listen to what he just heard a little while ago, then shouts out to him as a warning, "Listen Aziz, the next time I see you with that dishonest young man, the punishment will be severe." At that point, Aziz is hit with a violent shock like he has never felt before. He spends his remaining hours at work in a confused state of mind, with troubled feelings and thoughts, and at the end of the night, he goes to that miserable bar in Bab al-Khadra and drinks two or three beers, and then goes back to his apartment, cursing the human beings who profess innocence and kindness when they are in fact chameleons who change their colors according to circumstances and interests. Before lying down to sleep, he swears to God most high and most powerful over and over again that if I ever went up to him as if everything was hunky-dory he would spit in my face, and warn me of the consequence of getting close to him ever again.

That's right, that was the scenario I imagined in my mind after the relationship between Hajj Marzouq and those scumbags grew stronger, so I hurried to quit working there. I worried anew about my reputation in the big city, avoiding all the places where I might find myself face to face with Aziz.

During my long walks, many ideas appeared one after another in my mind. But the idea of "burning" off to Italy preoccupied me more than any other ideas. In the end, I couldn't get the idea out of my head and it remained present in my dreams and nightmares. I started following with interest in the newspapers and on television any news of the burners from my country or from Africa or people from the East fleeing wars and corrupt regimes. I won't deny that I panicked when I saw the bodies of some of those burners washed up on the Italian and Spanish coastlines, so decomposed and bloated that it became difficult to determine their identities, but by and by everything became equal to me, and I started telling myself that death at the bottom of the sea is better than living among the scumbags of M Slum and begging in the streets with empty pockets on an empty stomach. Maybe because of the continuous wandering without a defined goal, my imagination expanded, and I saw myself facing the boundless countries of the east that had been scorched by wars and conflicts. If I survived the death that had become an everyday occurrence there, I would be able to cross the deserts and the oceans in order to reach the lands of India and the city of Delhi, with its great wall that has no equal throughout the lands of Islam, and then I would vist the grave of that shaykh mentioned by Ibn Battuta who used to present bits of silver and gold to people like me who were in a state of despair and frustration. Afterward I'd turn toward Kul, and from there go on to the state of Abad, then to the lands of Malabar, or the "lands of pepper," as Ibn Battuta calls them. Afterward I'd get lost among those wondrous islands where once a month a gigantic demon appears, forcing the people to leave, uttering *la ilaha illa Allah* and *Allahu akbar*, the children stand up with Qurans on their heads for protection. As for the women, they bang on copper pots so the demon won't bring them any harm. I was still lost among those distant islands, discovering their secrets and the circumstances of their people, when Aziz stopped me while I was walking near Bab al-Saadoun in the direction of the municipal prison.

"Hey . . . Is that you?" he shouted, touching me as though he wasn't certain that I wasn't me. Then he added, "Where've you been? I've been looking all over for you for weeks!"

"I've been sick."

He stared at me hard, then said, "I don't see a trace of illness on your face."

"I told you, I've been sick. But I'm better now."

"And why haven't you shown up for work if you're better now?"

"Hajj Marzouq doesn't want me there anymore."

Aziz stared at me disapprovingly and then said, "That's just not true. Hajj Marzouq went to ask my uncle about you more than once. He praised you, he extolled your morals, and your qualities at work. He asked me to look for you as well."

Anxiety left my heart. In secret I thanked God that those despicable guys hadn't succeeded in carrying out the hellish plot they had been planning against me. Nevertheless, I told Aziz, "I'm sure Hajj Marzouq doesn't want me anymore."

"What proof do you have of what you are saying?"

"He started being mean to me. Sometimes he even insulted me in front of the customers. That's something I can't tolerate. "

Aziz became infuriated and shouted at me, "What you're saying simply isn't true! You must go back to work at once to see just how much Hajj Marzouq regards and respects you!"

"I'm not going back," I said with plain insistence.

Aziz remained silent for a while, then said, "And what do you intend to do?"

"I'll look for another job."

"Fine, do whatever you want. But don't forget that I still consider you a dear friend and don't want anything but the best for you."

Aziz said that in a vanquished tone and then left without saying goodbye. I remained standing there, watching him as he walked away, and pain squeezed my heart and my entire being. The next morning, after a troubled night, I went to Hafsia to inform Aziz that I had decided to go back to work at the café and, just then, he embraced me, delighted and congratulatory. He accompanied me as far as Bab al-Bahr. Before leaving me, he placed his right hand on my shoulder and, with his eyes on mine, said, "Listen to me Alaa al-Din, I know that working in a café isn't for you. You're a smart guy, you have decent skills and abilities that might be beneficial in another field. But be patient, my friend, because God brings the ultimate freedom, isn't that right?"

"You're right," I said.

I went back to work. Those scumbags came back to make my life miserable almost every day, and my soul grew black once again. Steering clear of their evil, I found myself forced to leave al-Salam Café to work at a bar in Lafayette. One evening they showed up right in front of me. They were drunk, talking and staggering, collapsing onto the chairs. My father's murderer raised his voice and shouted at me, "You, boy, get us five beers now!"

At that moment, the world went dark before my eyes and I left the bar to wander aimlessly around the city until morning. During that night, the loneliest of my life, I resolved to take action, and to relax. Up until the day of the event, I avoided seeing Aziz for fear that he might talk me out of what I intended to do. In fact, he was capable of talking me out of it even if he didn't know what was running around in my mind. . . .

THE MOTHER

Please don't insult me and say that I was delusional, that I was only imagining Mansour would give me the life I had always desired and dreamed about, a life that was all softness and comfort and convenience, that he was going to install me in a beautiful house in a respectable neighborhood, and that he was going to do this or that for me. That's why I married him in such a hurry and without any hesitation, as though I were a young lady who remained anxious about being unmarriageable. No, no, no. Shame on you for thinking such thoughts about me. I knew full well that I was about to marry a railway worker who had denied himself the pleasures of life that young men of his age usually accepted in order to buy a simple house in a modest working-class neighborhood. I've already confessed to you that I married him without love, and that the primary objective in my marrying him was getting out of that dirt-poor village that had made my life into daily torture, haunted by nighttime and daytime nightmares in which I would see myself looking out over a shadowy ravine, and from behind me a hand reaches out about to push me into the depths. But my good people, I never dreamed of suddenly finding myself in a cramped, poorly built house on the edge of the railroad tracks, which I learned later on was the line connecting Bizerte with the capital. And believe me, as soon as I entered the house after an arduous journey in an old crowded bus, on an extremely hot day, I felt the desire to go right back where I had come from. I remember that I spent the first night crying over my bad luck, and I only slept a little bit. As for Mansour, he washed up, ate half the chicken he had bought on the way, and fell into a deep sleep until morning. The first few months were the most difficult and bitter times I knew in my entire life. Mansour would go to work at dawn and wouldn't return until just before sundown. As for me, I used to spend the day in that cramped, dreary house. When I looked out into the street, whether from the door or through one of the windows, I recoiled, my entire body shaking with fear. The faces staring back at me reflected either the souls of tortured, deprived, defeated, miserable, and helpless creatures, or the souls of fierce, agressive, contemptuous, conscienceless creatures. At night Mansour would devour his dinner in silence, and then sit down in front of the television to follow world news, still silent. At ten-thirty, he went to bed and left me all alone to listen to the night in the capital as he sighed deeply, weary of all those people. Sometimes, very late at night, the sounds of young men fighting would ring out, or of drunks coming home making bawdy comments, or of women fighting with their husbands. One day, as I ventured to leave the house in order to buy some salt and matches from the nearby pharmacist, eyes stared at me, as stunned and enraged as if they were both surprised by my very existence and disapproving of it at the same time. But by and by, I started to get to know the conditions of M Slum, to discover how most of its inhabitants were people who the hardship of life had forced to leave their small villages behind, to flood into the peripheries of the capital, like swarms of locusts searching for verdant lands during a time of famine and drought. Dreaming of a better life, they quickly found themselves having lost everything, and they remained lost creatures without origins or roots. Under the pressures of everyday life, its twists and turns and its raging storms, these creatures gave up all their human feelings and values. In those ugly neighborhoods where they piled up, they resorted to every way and every means, including crime and deception, lying and hypocrisy, and vice of every type and kind, in order to secure their daily bread. Those discoveries made me increasingly disgusted by M Slum and frustrated with living there. One night I exploded in rage and shouted in Mansour's face while he was following the world news in silence, as usual, "Listen to me, I'm not going to let you imprison me in this house all the time!"

"And just where do you want to go?"

"To the capital!"

"But you're in the capital already," he replied, the hint of a half-joking smile on his lips.

"No, I'm not in the capital. I'm in a filthy slum where I can't bear to live any longer!"

He was silent for a moment, watching a march in occupied Palestine, and then he said, "All right, tomorrow I'll take you to the capital."

The next afternoon, it was a Saturday, I put on my finest and most beautiful clothes, and accompanied Mansour on a long walk that started from Bab Suwayqa, then Sidi Mehrez, Suq al-Qarana, Suq al-Attarin, and, finally, Bab al-Bahr, and I won't hide the fact that once we arrived there, that is, in Bab al-Bahr, I wished I had been alone in order to stand for a long time in front of the clothing, perfume, and shoe stores, and to stare for a long time at the faces walking back and forth. Maybe I'd sit in one of those fancy cafés and have a coffee or an orange juice, watching the wide boulevard that pulsed with God's creation. Afterward I'd continue on my way at my own pace, under the trees, as the breeze coming off the sea played with the curls of my hair. During my journey, I noticed that Mansour was confused, uncomfortable. It seemed to me that he regretted accompanying me on this walk, and that what he might have been feeling during it was that he was a servant, not a husband. I won't deny the fact that lots of men, especially in the old city, were devouring me with their eyes as though I was the only woman they'd seen that day. There were some who had it written all over their faces how offended they were to see a woman with my physique and beauty and elegance walking beside a frail, modestly dressed man, hunched over slightly, who looked more than ten years over his age. In Bab al-Bahr, a young man of around thirty smiled at me and then proceeded to follow us. I think that Mansour noticed because I heard him say to me in a dry voice, "We're going home!" And we did. I was like a captive returned to the darkness of the cell after a brief respite out in the green and the light!

That night, Mansour wolfed down his dinner, then went to sleep without turning on the television, and without saying a single word to me. I continued listening to the night alone, as usual, thinking to myself, *You must save yourself, Najma, before it's too late. Wasn't Aunt Warda praying to God that you would always be like a pomegranate, delicious and full on the inside, attractive on the outside? So you must be like the pomegranate, but as long as you remain cooped up inside this cramped house, in this rancid, desolate slum filled with evil people and frustrated and despairing people, the pomegranate that you are is going to rot away and turn black from the inside out, and its rind will lose its distinctive color and dry up, becoming as solid as stone. That's right . . . that's how* it will be as long as you continue living your life in this awful way, in this frightening routine. Besides, you must know that the dirt-poor village you left behind isn't sorry, and after you paid such a high price, it's much better than the filthy slum you now live in. Would you consent to escape from hell, only to find yourself in an even worse hell? Well then, get a move on . . . get a move on, my dear Najma, before time does its terrible things to you and you find yourself one day having wilted, and gotten fat and dried up, when no one will turn to look at you, neither the old nor the young. Besides, do you really believe that the women of Bab al-Bahr are more beautiful than you? You're mistaken if you do. So get a move on and be like them, or better than them. Get a move on . . . please get a move on before it's too late . . . before it's too late!

THE SON

Before I was transferred to death row, the prison director asked me with
all good grace and manners if I wanted anything in particular, on the condition that it didn't violate the laws of the country, so I asked for the *Rihla*
of Ibn Battuta. Maybe he thought that the young man standing before
him, who presented such a request, couldn't possibly be the same man
who committed that monstrous crime near the Arches of Zaghouan, and
so the prison director stared at me for a few moments, astonished, before
muttering his approval of my request. Nevertheless, the features of his
flour-colored face, swollen up with flab, continued to intimate, without
a doubt, that this state of amazement and astonishment that had stricken
him upon my request would remain with him for a long time, quite possibly until after he had gone into retirement. From time to time he'll feel
like telling many people about the request that so amazed and astonished
him, especially those who work with him in the prison administration
and those who sneak away with him to play cards and smoke the nargileh
in the café that he frequents on his weekly day off, as well as his friends,
his wife, and his family members, because what he had heard was worth
writing in the gilded notebook he set aside especially for recording important events from the four decades he spent in the prison administration,
climbing the employment ladder one rung after another. I imagine him
addressing these people, saying in a pleasant mood, proud of the exten-
sive expertise he had acquired, "Do you remember that young man who
committed an awful crime near the Arches of Zaghouan, the one the

newspapers talked about so much, and whose case preoccupied the entire country for weeks, or even months?"

Stretching their necks out in his direction, they reply, "Ahh, yes. We remember him, we remember him. But hasn't he been executed already?"

"Yes, he was executed!" Mr. Director replies, then shifts his gaze away from them and plunges into silence, demonstrating to them how someone with a secret cannot easily divulge it to others. They all mutter something, perplexed. Silent, they fix their eyes upon him, hope flickering in them that he will reveal as much of his hidden secret as he is able.

Mr. Director lights a cigarette. After taking two or three puffs, he wheels around and says, "That's right. He's been executed. But do you know what he asked for back when he was being transferred to death row?"

They all shake their heads right and left twice in a row as a negative response.

Mr. Director takes another pull on his cigarette. For a moment in time he continues to follow the blue smoke rings floating up out of his nostrils, and then, staring at them one after another, like a teacher with students who can't answer an ambiguous question, says, "He asked for the *Rihla* of Ibn Battuta."

Here, ladies and gentleman, I would leave you to freely guess how what the director said affects those who were listening to him, but I think you're all uninterested in what I'm about to say. Rather, perhaps you're all making fun of me and scoffing at me, convinced I've lost my mind and started to babble and rave here in my dismal cell, displaying false courage in the face of imminent death. I might not be mistaken when I say that you are now whispering among yourselves, "What a pathetic young man. Obviously he doesn't know what he's saying anymore and has started to rant and rave without even realizing it. Why else would he insist on having us believe that the *Rihla* of Ibn Battuta was the only request he presented to the prison administration before being transferred to his cell on death row?" Even more alert and intelligent than all of you, who you have grown accustomed to consulting whenever circumstances and matters in affairs of the world and society are unclear to you, Mr. Director stands up and, wagging his right index finger right and left, tells you, "No. No. You don't understand what the young man actually meant."

"So what did he mean?" you'll all ask him. And he replies, "That he wants to make you all believe he isn't the filthy criminal, the heartless unscrupulous criminal you all think he is, but rather, that he's just a human being, one who's even acquired a certain amount of culture, but the harsh conditions he's had to endure are what made him lose his way, what forced him to commit that monstrous crime."

And you ask another time, "Does this mean that he wants us to take pity on him and show him mercy?"

"Yes, that's exactly what he wants!"

You all get excited and rebel as if I were standing right there in front of you, and you all shout at me, enraged, waving your hands in the air, "No. Never! We can neither take pity on you nor show you any mercy. We cannot. We can't. We can't!"

And you may say even more violent and severe things than that. At any rate, you are all free to say and do whatever you like. But rest assured, ladies and gentlemen, that I don't intend, through what I've said or what I'm going to say, to make you believe anything, and I, who am going to the gallows in a day or so, don't want you to be merciful with me, to show me any sympathy. No. No. I don't want this from you at all. Not at all. The one thing I do want from you is to hear me out. This is all I ask of you. And rest assured that I have not said and will not say anything untrue until the end of my story.

That's right, ladies and gentlemen. I really did ask for the *Rihla* of Ibn Battuta before being transferred to my cell on death row. I had read that travel narrative when I was sixteen years old, and because it comforted me and afforded me a kind of pleasure that no other book could, I re-read its chapters more than once. As a result, many of its details were lodged in my memory. I think requesting it was the best thing I could have done. In my cell it became my most intimate friend and greatest sitting companion. With its author, I get lost in God's wide country. No borders, no customs. Just lands that lead to other lands that might be more beautiful or more unsightly. A desert bids you farewell as you find yourself in another desert, one more spacious and more terrifying. You become comfortable in an ocean before it suddenly tosses you into another ocean, where the storms seem to never stop around the clock. Cities receive you with cheers and roses, while others prevent you from entering, slamming their seven gates in your face. Wonders and marvels that perplex the mind lead you to other wonders and marvels that would put gray hair on a baby's head. Adventures sweep you away to other adventures as you find yourself face to face with creatures who you can't tell whether they're human or jinn.

I calmly flipped through the pages of the book. Here I am in the great port of Alexandria that has no equal among all the ports of the world except for the ports of Kulm and Calicut in India, the port of Kaffa in Turkey, and the port of Zaytoun in the lands of China. There I am in the ruins of the ancient cities of Greater Syria. And there I am crossing the Red Sea to visit the Holy Land. Afterward I cross the desert into Iraq, and from there I head toward the lands of Persia, continuing my journey by land and by sea until I look out over the most distant land, from where the sun rises.

But I must confess to all of you that what most attracted me to the *Rihla* of Ibn Battuta were those tales that stand your hair up on end, those that reveal the evil hidden within the human being, in particular his cruelty and harshness toward his fellow man. In all the lands he passed through, Ibn Battuta came across injustices and acts and secrets that the imagination cannot visualize: he saw innocent people being slaughtered, crucified in the markets and on the gates of the cities, an example made out of them in broad daylight, without anyone being bothered by them. In the lands of the Mughals, Ibn Battuta saw a minaret constructed out of the skulls and heads of those killed by the ruler of that realm, all of whom had opposed his oppression and tyranny. There were tales that I always re-read, including the one about a Muslim sultan in the lands of China. This sultan slaughters the wives of infidels, killing all the children in their care. One day, this sultan was eating his lunch with the judge and with Ibn Battuta, when the guards appeared with an infidel, his wife, and their seven-year old child. He immediately instructed the executioners to behead the infidel, and to behead his wife and child as well. The territories of this sultan neighbored lands ruled by an infidel sultan, and in spite of the fact that the latter possessed a gargantuan army, the Muslim sultan was able to inflict an ignominious defeat upon him, and then imprison him. In order to acquire riches and elephants and horses from him, he praised him in public and assaulted him in private, but as soon as he had gotten what he wanted out of him, he killed him and skinned him, stuffing his skin with straw and then stringing him up from the ramparts. But hold on for a moment, ladies and gentlemen, I didn't call your attention to atrocities such as these for some unknown reason, but in order to urge you to go back to his *Rihla* if you've read it before, or to read it if you haven't done so up until this hour, so that you will realize that history has been this frightening since the time of the pharaohs and up until the day of these people.

Now then, allow me to surprise you by saying that my grandmother, may God's vast mercy be upon her and may He install her in the paradises of His heavens, was a lot like Ibn Battuta and, like him, she used to tell wondrous tales that would make those who listened to them stay up late into the night, and I was one of them. The only difference between her and Ibn Battuta was that she used to travel only through her imagination to God's wide country, and it was with her imagination that she was able to whisk you away to Sind and to Hind, to the lands of terrors and ghouls, to the deserts where snakes fly from the intensity of the heat, to snow-capped mountains where a human being can freeze even while still walking, to islands inhabited by races of giants who subsist on human flesh, and to kingdoms ruled by tyrants who take pleasure in setting starving lions loose upon dissidents and all those who conspire against them, even servants who make small mistakes. That's right, my grandmother was capable of all that. When I discovered Ibn Battuta, I remembered her, and I cried in agony since I so would have liked to talk to her about him, but she had already been buried in the ground for more than a year.

Ah, Grandma! I remember that she died at the end of an autumn that had grown so lonely, filled with dust and flies. Anyone who touched her body upon the moment of final farewell would swear that she was as hot as an ember. Maybe she remained like that until she was interred in the earth. My grandmother was an exceptional woman, always moving and active in her youth, as well as in middle and old age. Like a wild rabbit, she used to sleep with one eye closed, leaving the other one open. Even when she surpassed seventy years of age, her life went on just as it had been when she was a young lady who whinnied like a mare. Not even once did her family ever see her in need of help or assistance. She continued to insist on personally attending to her own affairs, unlike the other old women who would spend their time hunched over like sick animals. My grandmother was getting ready to embark upon her weekly journey back to the village when the angel of death sprang upon her. She had retained her vitality and clarity of mind right up until the very last moment of her life—that was why she went to the grave as warm as an ember. The thing that really got to me then, and tortures me still, that pained me and still pains me, wasn't just her sudden death, but the fact that I didn't attend her funeral. My mother, who had gone, only rarely ever talked about it, and then only with extreme brevity, as if the departed wasn't her mother. As though I wasn't her grandson who she loved more than all the other grandchildren for a reason known only to me. She would greet me with tears of joy, and bid me farewell with tears of sorrow; she would hold me with a tenderness I hadn't known from anyone except my father. When she took me with her on those journeys around the village and out into the olive and almond groves she would say pleasant words to me that I'd never heard the likes of from anyone else, not even from my father, who was a taciturn man, whose great love for me and whose pride in me as an only child I didn't sense except through the hurling expressions that used to be stamped on his sallow face and in his sad eyes. Those words were like salve on the wounds that were opened up in my heart and soul by the curses and mocking words that the people of the filthy M Slum used to hurl at me. Perhaps the most wonderful image I have of my grandmother is the one that has been lodged in my memory since I was eight years old. It was the end of summer. I had fallen asleep beside her after she told me one of those tales that used to make me happy and delight me more than anything else in the world. Perhaps I was still drowning in the surroundings of a beautiful dream when I opened my eyes to see my grandmother merging with the red dawn out on the distant horizon. Standing up and then bending over prostrate, she appeared to me as if she were a floating black cloud adorned with marvelous lights. Overcome with terror, I remained frozen in bed. Just then, I raised my voice, calling for my grandmother, but she didn't respond. I imagined she was drawing away from me, and I broke down in tears. At that moment, I felt her warm tender hand on my forehead, and I heard her say, "Don't be afraid, my son . . . I'm right here beside you!" And she truly was there beside me. Only then did I realize that she hadn't drawn away from me as I had imagined in the dim light separating night from day, but rather that she had been praying in front of the door open upon the horizon speckled with the red of rising dawn.

As I already mentioned, my grandmother was a river that never ran dry of stories. She would tell each story in such a way that allowed you to experience its events and its surprises from beginning to end, as if you were one of its characters. I must declare that my grandmother's stories were what helped me tolerate prison and its daily tortures. I had learned a decent number of those stories by heart, but the tale of Alaa al-Din in the Land of Terrors always was and still remains my favorite, so I asked my grandmother on a number of occasions, practically begging, to tell it to me. She used to honor my request without any hesitation, saying, "I love that story too. Maybe that's why I named you after its hero, Alaa al-Din.

"So listen up—come one come all, hear ye hear ye, God guides us and guides you to see. Once upon a time, long, long ago, there was a desert prince, who had three elegant palaces with scores of servants, and vast oases with plenty of the finest things on earth, and twenty purebred horses. His merchant caravans would travel from north to south, from east to west, carrying all manner of goods. Nonetheless, this prince wasn't happy with his life. He had married three beautiful women, but they were all barren. This situation agonized the prince and kept him awake many nights. And so it was that the prince was tortured and remained sleepless, preoccupied throughout the night, and solemn, distracted all day long. This situation continued to press upon him so much that he sometimes failed to hear what was said to him, failing to notice what was going on all around him except on rare occasions. In their seclusion, his wives would implore God, crying and complaining about their deprivation from having children, the adornment of life in this world. One day, when the prince was sitting out in the oasis thinking to himself, contemplating the misfortunes of both past and present, tracing lines in the sand with his staff that reflected the anxieties of his troubled and tortured soul, there appeared before him a dignified and venerable-looking stranger. He was wearing a gleaming-white robe and shoes of the same color, with a red tarboosh on his graying head. The stranger greeted the prince warmly, but the prince returned his greeting with chilliness. Once again he bowed his head, and started to stare at the lines he had drawn in the sand, as if he was trying to deduce from them the meanings they might symbolize. Without asking for permission, the stranger sat down in front of the prince and asked him, 'What are you thinking about, O prince?'

"Without lifting his head, the prince replied, 'By God, stranger, leave me in peace. This concern that has been tormenting me for so many years has no cure as far as I can tell up until this hour, and it seems that there's nothing in this whole wide world that can help me be rid of it.'

"The stranger was silent for a moment and then said, smiling, 'But prince, God has accorded you many of His finest blessings, and blessed you with wealth and with life, so how can it be that He has been stingy with you in terms of what might relieve you of this concern you say has tormented you for many years?'

"The prince raised his head. He stared for a long time into the dignified face of the stranger that radiated wisdom and intelligence, and said, 'It's true that God has accorded me many of his finest blessings and blessed me with wealth and with life, but He has deprived me of the one thing without which those blessings and this wealth and this life are meaningless!'

"'And what is that?' the stranger asked him, smiling.

"'Ahh . . . something that concerns me and me alone. I can't reveal it to anyone!' the prince replied in a sharp tone, as though he wanted to end the conversation between him and the stranger right then and there. But the stranger moved in closer to the prince and, with great affection, as that smile spread further across his face, said, 'Don't you trust me?'

"'How can I trust a stranger I've only just met?'

"The two men carried on like that, in fits and starts. Finally, after convincing himself that strangers could be trusted to guard secrets even more than those with whom we have durable relationships, the prince revealed his secret to the stranger. Without giving any indication of surprise at what he had heard, the stranger, growing ever more serious and dignified, said, 'But this matter is quite easy and simple, O prince!'

"The prince stood up as if a fire had been lit underneath him. For a few moments his mouth gaped wide open, his vision glazed over like someone struck by lightning, and then, as if posing a question to himself, he asked, 'A matter quite easy and simple?'

"'That's right . . . a matter quite easy and simple!' replied the stranger, who then handed the prince three apples in a sack; the prince had no idea where the stranger had been hiding them all this time. The stranger added, 'Give one apple to each of your wives, and God will achieve for you what you have desired for many years!'

"'That's all there is to it?' asked the prince, growing increasingly astonished and amazed.

"'Yes, that's all there is to it . . . but I have one condition you must accept or else the apples won't work, in fact, they might even harm the health of your wives!'

"'And what's the condition?' the prince asked, distressed.

"'That you hand over to me one of your sons. I require that it be the first-born and I give you my word that I will let him visit you once a year.'

"The prince got dispirited. The cloud of that old concern came back to cover his face. At a loss, he watched the stranger as he said, 'That's my only condition. If you won't accept it, then I bid you good day . . . .' Then he made as if to get up and leave. But the prince stopped him with a wave from his hand, 'Stay a moment!'

"After a short silence, the prince asked, 'Won't you give me some time to think it over?'

"'That's not possible,' the stranger responded resolutely.

"The prince bowed his head in thought and then, like a helpless man, said, 'You shall have this from me!'"

At this point my grandmother would stop. In the spacious garden of the house, illuminated by stars of the summer night, charming in its beauty, she would look as though she had never belonged to our world, but rather was part of the world of fairytales which she loved using her imagination to get lost in. Just then, my grandmother would start up the story of Alaa al-Din in the Land of Terrors anew, saying, "And in fact, just as that stranger predicted, God achieved for the prince what he had been wishing for over a period of many years, bestowing upon him three sons who lit up his life and his palace with their handsomeness and beauty. He named the first-born Alaa al-Din. Delighted by this joyous occasion, parties and celebrations were held. Visitors came from all over to congratulate him, blessing the occasion. In all of that exuberance, the prince forgot all about the stranger, and he didn't remember him until life had returned to its normal pace. But the matter didn't preoccupy him very often. Gazing upon his children as they matured before his very eyes, he felt that it wouldn't be easy for anyone in the world to deprive him of the happiness God had obtained for him. And by and by, the prince ceased to remember the stranger, except on rare occasions. If he did remember him at all, it was as a specter belonging to the world of imagination, not the world of reality.

"And as you all well know—come one come all, hear ye hear ye, God guides us and guides you to see—children in fairy tales grow up very fast. The children of the prince grew up, studied with the best teachers, memorized the word of God and the poems of the ancients, and started to master the art of horsemanship and hunting and other things. Their father was proud of them, overseeing their education, making certain to satisfy their requests, whether it was easy for him or difficult. Alaa al-Din was more intelligent and charming than his two brothers. He was superior to them at horsemanship and hunting, and he had a sweeter tongue, so the elders used to love talking to him, and they all wanted to debate him about many sacred and secular matters as well as other things. When he honored their desire, he displayed broad erudition and sagacity that was rare among those his age.

"It so happened that Alaa al-Din, who used to enjoy some solitude, went out one afternoon to take a walk in his father's orchards. The weather was spring-like and the world was in full bloom. When he grew tired of walking around, he sat down underneath a tree to rest. Soon he nodded off to sleep. When he opened his eyes, he saw before him a man with a solemn appearance, gray covering his hair. He was gazing upon him with fatherly affection.

"Alaa al-Din stood up, and the stranger asked him, smiling, 'Are you Alaa al-Din, son of the prince?'

"'Yes, I am he,' Alaa al-Din replied.

"'I'm glad to meet you,' said the stranger.

"Then he introduced himself, saying that he was an old friend of the prince, a perpetual traveler who hated living in a single place. Then he started talking about all the lands he had visited, about the princes and the great merchants whom he had met during his many travels. When Alaa al-Din desired to leave, the stranger told him, 'I beg of you to convey my warmest greetings to your father, the prince, and tell him that the owner of the three apples would like him to honor the promise he made fifteen years ago.'

"But Alaa al-Din, preoccupied with many other things during those days, forgot to tell his father. The same thing happened after his second encounter with the stranger. As usual he had been walking around alone in the afternoon. Upon their third meeting, the stranger grew more severe, and seemed determined to scold him who had thought little of him and his covenant. But Alaa al-Din, who was accustomed to being brave and sure of himself, especially around those who try to belittle him, wasn't affected by the stranger's anger, shouting at him defiantly, 'If you say that you're an old friend of my father's, why not go see him yourself and speak with him directly about this matter!'

"'That's none of your business!' the stranger shouted, growing increasingly enraged and malevolent.

"'If this matter is none of my business, please leave me alone and don't get in my way again, or else the punishment will be severe!'

"At that moment, black covered up all of existence, and storms and thunder rumbled, and Alaa al-Din sensed that raging winds were lifting him way up high. When he tried to shout for help, his voice got trapped in his throat, and he continued flying through the cold darkness, as the winds played with him like an autumn leaf. Then, suddenly, he was thrown to the ground like an apple core, and at that moment, the storms died down and the winds quieted, and the darkness was swept away. Just then, Alaa al-Din found himself in a high-walled fortress, with thick metal gates. It was gray and desolate, devoid of all signs of life, as if it were inhabited by an eternal winter. From time to time, black crows would pass over the fortress, beating the sky with their wings, making ominous sounds, and hurling threats and menaces. Just then, the stranger appeared before Alaa al-Din in a frightening, terrifying form, with malice on his frowning face and sparks shooting out of his eyes. With a voice like thunder before a storm breaks, the man said, 'I am the King of Shadows and from now on you are my prisoner. You won't ever get out of this fortress and nobody will be able to find you, so don't even think about escaping . . . and don't try deceiving me or lying to me or you'll wind up dead!'

"Then the stranger told Alaa al-Din what had happened between him and his father fifteen years earlier. Afterward he added, 'I'll come back at the end of every month . . . in the fortress you'll find all the food and clothing you need. You can open up all of the rooms except one, so you won't find its key among those I'm going to leave for you.'"

My grandmother would stop talking again, and ask me, "Do you want to hear more?"

Sleep would have been tempting me for some time, but I would cling to the fringes of her olive-colored shawl, and say, "I don't want to go to sleep until after you finish the story, dear grandmother!"

"But the story is long and everyone in the village is asleep already except for us!"

"Yes, but I want to hear more, sweet grandmother!"

"All right . . . I'll go on, but I know I can't finish the story until tomorrow night."

Once again my grandmother would get lost in that wondrous world and I would get lost with her, forgetting all about M Slum, about all the torments I had been subjected to ever since opening my eyes upon the world. . . .

"At first—come one come all, hear ye hear ye, God guides us and guides you to see—Alaa al-Din cried in anguish like a little boy who finds himself suddenly separated from his family, deprived of the tenderness of his mother and father, locked up inside a gloomy empty fortress, and during the first seven days, he lost his appetite and his desire to sleep. Because of that, he was struck twice with nausea that made him fall down to the ground. It's true that he found in the fortress everything that was sweet and delicious from the bounty of the earth—fruit, meat, fish, milk, cheeses, clarified honey, assorted sweets. There were also warm plates that never got cold, and all of the rooms were very comfortable. There were beds in them suitable for children of princes like him and there were baths and perfumes and other things like that, but all of it seemed to have no taste and no meaning in the fortress of the King of Shadows, which was like an enormous tomb. By and by Alaa al-Din got a grip on himself, and started to exercise, especially in the morning right after he woke up, aiming to protect his physical well-being. When he found books in one room, he started setting aside hours for reading every day. In spite of all that, he wasn't able to forget about his family and his old life in which he used to wander through the fields in the afternoon, debating the elders about secular and sacred matters, playing games with his brothers that brought happiness and joy into their hearts, listening to his mother as she sang sweet songs to him, caressing his hair with her hand; therefore sorrow would press upon him from time to time, and he'd find himself crying like a little boy.

"One evening, Alaa al-Din was pacing in the courtyard of the fortress, thinking about where his life had taken him, when a raging storm broke out. Just then, the earth quaked beneath his feet, and the world went all black. Once silence and calm had returned, Alaa al-Din found himself facing the stranger. The truth is—come one come all, hear ye hear ye, God guides us and guides you to see—that the stranger didn't only have that one fortress where Alaa al-Din was locked away; rather, he had thirty fortresses and between each one of those fortresses there was a vast distance. Because he couldn't bear to live in one place, the stranger used to spend one night in each fortress, and then depart for another one with the speed of the wind, as if he were a jinn, but it was within his power to appear in the form of a dignified and wise human being when there was need for that. That was the form he took in front of Alaa al-Din's father on that afternoon when the latter was absorbed in his own concerns. With the exception of the fortress where Alaa al-Din was locked away, all the other fortresses were empty, there was nothing in their rooms except for skulls and bones and locked-up women who perished from the loneliness of solitude and their great longing for their family and relatives. Now this stranger, who really was a jinn, as I just told you, possessed an exceptional power to make barren women fertile. He actually made a great number of them pregnant, but he would place unfair conditions upon their husbands, and if they didn't satisfy them, he'd kidnap their sons or their daughters when they reached the age of maturity, and then lock them away in his fortresses. Whereas he would permit boys to roam around inside the fortress, moving from room to room, he used to keep girls locked in the forbidden rooms, but he never touched them, not even lightly. He would suffice with looking at their feminine charms and inhaling their breaths for hours on end. It appears that the time has come for me to say to you all—come one come all, hear ye hear ye, God guides us and guides you to see—that Alaa al-Din wasn't alone in that fortress; rather, there was an exceptionally beautiful princess named Shayma in there with him. She, too, was the child of a desert prince. The stranger had stolen her away from her family just a few days before kidnapping Alaa al-Din, locking her away in the forbidden room. . . ."

At this point my grandmother stops, and stroking my hair with her tender hand, with me nearly incapable of opening my eyes, she says, "But, my dear grandson . . . I wonder, will Alaa al-Din discover the secret of the forbidden room? And will he be able to escape with Princess Shayma from that desolate fortress? You'll find out tomorrow night. . . ."

THE MOTHER

In my nightmares a raven and an owl are cawing atop ruins, and abandoned houses that have no doors or windows are filled with the dust of the yellow desert. Giant rats with their stomachs split open are strewn about the desolate wasteland, as hideous bald men run after me cackling loudly, exposing their repulsive genitals, and women with their eyes gouged out, without any hair, teeth, or breasts and with talons like birds of prey threaten to kill me, howling like starving wolves. Sometimes I see myself naked, my hands and feet bound, as the people of M Slum prepare to throw me into a roaring fire. I'm screaming and begging for help but nobody hears me, nobody cares. Because of all this, I become as terrified of night's approach as I had always been of the coming of the day. Mansour comes and goes, uninterested in me. He doesn't speak much. He always looks away from me, like a child who has made a mistake and is unable to look his father or his mother or any grownups in the eye. His only pleasure is in watching the news and Egyptian or Mexican soap operas. He watches them silently, frozen in place. If only he would make a movement or a sound even once, crack a smile or flash his teeth, anything at all that might indicate whether or not he's optimtistic about what he's seeing and hearing. He goes to bed at ten p.m. with exertion and exhaustion written all over him, as his face becomes even more shriveled and wan, his back ever more curved. Sometimes he looks like a seventy-year-old man. When he fucks me, I am gripped by the feeling that a vile beetle is crawling all over my flesh, and I long to kick him off of me once and for all.

Early in the morning he would go to work as silent and somber as if he were off to a mourning ceremony, leaving me home all alone, a stranger in that miserable fucking slum filled with evil men and women who made an art out of tormenting me and insulting me. If I took so much as a single step out into the street they would start up with their sardonic laughs, bawdy comments, and offensive expressions. My neighbor, that washed-up whore who was always sitting outside her front door as though she had been assigned to guard the neighborhood, who had eyes like a skittish puppy, loved saying, whenever she saw me, "May God protect your beauty and keep it intact!" After letting out a lewd laugh, the other neighbor, the globular one with an ass that weighed a ton, would weigh in, "But there will come a day when beauty fades, when it goes *troof troof* and breaks like a jar, and God have mercy upon anyone who tries to pick up the pieces." The washed-up whore replies, "Inshallah, from your mouth to God's ear, Suad, my dear." From the force of my confusion, I had trouble walking. The world would go black all around me and, just then, it was as if I were walking through darkness. They never quit making trouble for me. Even their children started getting fresh with me whenever I passed by them playing soccer or resting their backs against the walls, as they always and eternally seemed to be doing in their spare time.

Until one day I finally decided to do something.

I hailed a taxi and asked the elderly driver to take me to Bab al-Bahr. They were dumbstruck to see me leaving the house wearing make-up and dressed in my finest clothes, as if I was going to a wedding. This time, not one of them uttered a single world. Maybe the defiance and the determination stamped on my face that glorious morning held their wicked tongues in check. They just kept on staring at me, young and old, men and women alike, their mouths agape as though they were watching a princess on a big movie screen. I got out in the heart of Bab al-Bahr. It was winter but the weather was mild and the sun was shining in the sky without a single scattered white cloud. I began to stroll at my leisure. I had only taken a few steps when I felt my old self renewed. There I was, once again, carefree Najma, the tease, the flirt, the seductress, the joker, the lover of life. As I walked, the breeze off the sea played with my soft hair cascading down over my shoulders. I strolled unaffected by the devouring stares of all those men, by the women who stopped to stare at me, blinded by my beauty. I walked along. Occasionally I stoped outside this or that store, then continued on my way, always at my own pace. Happy. My mind was at peace. I walked, and walked, and the miserable fucking M Slum seemed like a nightmare irreversibly come to life. If I got tired, I would sit down in a swanky café where many women gathered. I ordered some orange juice. I wished I had a newspaper with me. In that moment I'd cross one leg over the other and drown in reading it like all the other respectable ladies. The idea soothed me, so I smiled, and the handsome thirty-something man who was sitting not too far away from me smiled back at me, thinking that my smile had been directed at him. I turned my face away. No, no, no. I hadn't gone out to hunt for men nor so men could hunt me. I just wanted to be myself. And there I was, feeling for the first time since arriving in the capital like I was that Najma I had nearly forgotten about and who had almost forgotten about me in that rancid slum, among those malevolent creatures who loved to feast on each other's flesh as if there were nothing else to do in the whole world.

Then I started to walk again. I walked along, and the wintry day became increasingly brilliant and resplendent. I forgot all about M Slum and its people and its nightmares and Mansour. All of that seemed to me like something from a distant past that had faded in my memory. But the days in winter are short, as you know, and just like that, in a flash, the luminous light started to fade away and die, and darkness began to descend, cold, as dark clouds appeared in the sky. I took a taxi and went home to cry in agony, like a prisoner who was able to enjoy a few hours of freedom but must then be returned once again to their gloomy and depressing cell.

THE SON

My grandmother didn't like to tell her wondrous tales during the day-time. She confidently told me that those who did so could be struck with blindness and possibly other dangerous debilities that can even be passed down to their offspring, who might be born deformed, so I would spend the length of the day on the coals of anticipation. When night fell and the village went to sleep, making it so quiet you could hear a needle fall into a haystack, I would sit down beside my grandmother as she started to caress my hair absent-mindedly and then immediately took me with her to that vast magical world, the world of fairytales.

But ladies and gentlemen, I want to let you know that I'm not going to continue the tale of Alaa al-Din in the Land of Terrors right now, not because it's too long, and not because half the night has passed already, because neither sleep nor time concerns me anymore, but rather, in order to afford you all the opportunity of having the same experience that I had. Now as I've already told you, I would keep trying to figure out, from morning until the onset of night, how would Alaa al-Din ever be able to get out of that terrible fortress? How was he going to get around the deadly dangers he was going to have to face in the Land of Terrors and Ghouls? And, finally, was luck going to help him make it safe and sound back to his home after such a long absence? I won't hide the fact that I used to let my imagination run wild as I tried to figure out the answer to all the questions burning me up inside, but my imagination always came up empty, devoid of anything that might help me put out those flames.

Only my grandma could decipher these most ambiguous and obscure talismans and riddles. Over time I came to realize that nobody discovers the secret of the story except the one who possesses its keys. My grandmother possessed the keys to every tale she ever told, so it was impossible for anyone but her to know the details of the chapters yet to come! Try your luck, just try and answer the questions I just posed. I'm sure that none of you will come up with anything, no matter how weak.

Not only had my grandmother perfected the telling of fairytales, but also she was skilled and successful in pleasing people with stories from the fabric of reality, and from the fabric of her life in particular. She had also memorized precise details about people who had passed away a long time before; about thieves who used to raid the villages on cold winter nights; about explorers who used to cross vast distances barefoot, unafraid of the scorpions and the snakes and the thorns; about young men who were whisked away to wars that were being waged in European lands and who never came back; about her uncle Salih, who made the pilgrimage to the holy house of God on foot, then returned on foot as well; about someone named al-Kilani, who was capable of eating an entire goat and then asking, "Is there any more?"; and about Mabrouka the witch who would prepare couscous with the hands of the dead in order to deaden the hearts of men who were harsh toward women.

Among the most beautiful tales that I still have memorized in its entirety is the one my grandmother used to tell about the coming of the Germans to the village during the Second World War. She would start, "It was a dry year, among the most miserable and punishing years we ever lived, as the elders of our village insisted to us. The yellow dust storms were hitting us at least once a month, blanketing the horizon and filling our eyes and our ears and our noses and our houses with dirt. Because of the dryness of the soil, the livestock were subsisting on straw and thistles. In every house, supplies were running out with terrifying speed.

"On that sad autumn night, I was playing with my cousins near our house. The elders of the village were congregated in front of the olive press talking about the drought that had spread panic in the people's hearts, and about the war that had started getting closer, which we heard, day and night, as the boom of the artillery guns shook the mountains to the north and the plains to the south. Shaykh Salim al-Ahmar was successful in gathering information, therefore everyone would listen with great interest to every word he said. Suddenly there appeared out of the south

95

an enormous clay-colored barrel that proceeded to roll on chains, advancing toward the olive press. We all stopped playing, and the elders stopped talking, astonished, silent, as they watched the approach of the strange barrel that stopped moving once it had reached the olive press. From on top, three blond, blue-eyed men wearing wide-brimmed hats looked out at us. At first they communicated to the elders with gestures, then Abdel Aziz, who had served in the French army for many years, started communicating with them using what few French words he had learned. We soon learned that those blond men were German officers who had been in the desert and that they wanted to buy a chicken and some eggs. They also asked whether any American troops had passed through our village that day or any time before. They were so well mannered and gentle that fear was wiped from the people's hearts in those first moments they communicated with the elders. After buying some eggs and chickens, they disappeared once again inside the barrel that Abdel Aziz one day told us was called a 'tank.' We remained standing there, young and old, behind the olive press, monitoring its movement until it disappeared out of our sight in the valley separating us from the Sabba clan."

My grandmother loved to visit the graves of God's holy saints. She used to believe that every visit to every grave had baraka, which came with many benefits for the heart and soul and body. She had a particular affection for Sidi Abu al-Hasan al-Shadhili and she used to talk about him a great deal, especially during the month of Ramadan, and during the harvests and religious holidays. She would say, "Sidi Abu al-Hasan al-Shadhili has boundless and immeasurable baraka, his memory spread among Bedouins and settled people, among the people of the Maghreb and the people of the Mashreq. His words and his preaching smell of perfume, as though they were a bouquet of flowers in the spring, and his face would radiate a light that only radiated from the faces of those for whom God had obtained His generosity and His blessings. Those who were in the know would say that if Sidi Abd al-Qadir al-Gilani were mentioned, then Sidi Abu al-Hasan al-Shadhili must also be mentioned. He is from Morocco.... He used to wear wool.... He traveled in the countries of the East, especially in Iraq. There he met a venerable sheikh and told him, 'I've come from my distant country to seek your wisdom!' The venerable sheikh replied, 'Go back to your country where you will find the person that you seek!' So he took his advice and went back to his country. One day, he went up into tall mountains, the Rif Mountains. There in its heights he met a pious saint named Sidi Abdel Salam bin Bashish, with whom he spent a few days, during which time he saw and lived all manner of wonders. Sidi Abdel Salam bin Bashish advised him to go to Tunis. When he arrived there, still a young man, he found the people there dying of hunger and the markets full of dead bodies, and he thought to himself, 'If I had the money to buy bread for these starving people, I'd do it!' Then he heard a voice say to him, 'Use what's in your pocket!' So he put his hand in his pocket and, miraculously, there were dirhams inside. So he went to a breadmaker and asked him to make some bread. When he handed it out to the people, they grabbed for it. When he pulled out the dirhams, the breadmaker refused them and accused him of duplicity and counterfeiting. Sidi al-Hasan al-Shadhili hastily handed him his burnoos robe and shashiya cap in exchange for the bread and headed for the door. Just then, a man who had been standing there asked him, 'Where are those dirhams you had?' He handed them over. The man shook them in his hand and then handed them back, saying, 'Now go pay the breadmaker with them, they're not fake,' and he did just that. At that moment, the breadmaker said, 'These dirhams are good,' and gave him back the burnoos robe and the shashiya cap. But when he left, he didn't find the man who had shaken the coins in his hand. He remained perplexed until Friday. Upon entering the mosque to pray, he found the man sitting in the eastern corner and, when he greeted him, the man smiled and said, 'You said that if you had the money to feed those hungry people you would do it. Do you have the generosity of God in His act of creation? If He wanted to He could nourish them, for God is knowledgeable of their best interests.' Sidi Abu al-Hasan al-Shadhili asked him, 'Sir, by God who are you?' He told him, 'I'm Ahmad al-Khidr. I was once in China, where I was told, *Find a saint in Tunisia* . . . and so I've come to you.' After the Friday prayer, Sidi Abu al-Hasan al-Shadhili looked for the man again, but didn't find a trace of him."

My grandmother Umnia, which means 'wish,' had always wished to visit the shrine of Sidi Abu al-Hasan al-Shadhili, but she died without her wish coming true. On the commemoration of her arbaeen, I climbed the hill overlooking the capital and the al-Jalaz Cemetery, and I lit some candles in the shrine out of devotion to her pure heart. I spent nearly two hours there crying over her passing. When I hopped on the bus back to M Slum, I remembered that she said to me one day, "I'm afraid to leave this world, my dear grandson, without driving the Devil who seeks to ruin your life out of your soul!"

THE MOTHER

Please don't be too harsh with me, but don't be too merciful either. All I ask is that you not accuse me of ever having bad intentions, of messing around or lying, as the people of M Slum used to do, especially after I started dealing with them the way a person deals with vile insects. That's right, this is all I ask of you. Rest assured that I'll remain true to the promise I made from the start, and I'll never resort to fabrication, deception, changing the facts, or making things up, and I'll adhere to that until the end of my story, that is, until that blazing day on which I was transformed into ash in the ravine near the Arches of Zaghouan. Yes, that's just what I'm going to do, trust me!

The truth of the matter is that what happened to me is a lot like what happened to that young wife in the tale my mother used to tell people ever since I was a little girl and only knew very little about affairs of the world. The story goes that, once upon a time, long, long ago, there was a young lady, the news of whose beauty was rumored throughout districts both near and far. Because her husband was very jealous, his eyes were always on her, night and day. It so happened that a war broke out in the kingdom, and all the men of the small village where the young lady lived were called up to the front lines, including her husband, her three brothers, and her fifty-year-old father. Only the old men, women, and children remained, and that was how the young wife found herself forced not only to take care of household affairs, but the agricultural work and tending to the livestock, as well as looking after her disabled mother. Every day she would go to the spring to fetch drinking water. There were childish old men who were always sitting beneath the olive tree that overlooks the spring, sharing news of the war that was consuming all of the kingdom's land and produce. Whenever the young wife passed by, they would all start flirting with her, trying to attract her, and she would scold them, violently fighting them off. When all their attempts had yielded a resounding failure, they decided to come up with a plot against her. After a little more than a year, the war ended and all the men who were still alive returned home to the village. Fate chose the young wife's father, three brothers, and husband to be among them, and she was very happy about that, but she didn't receive anything except enmity and standoffishness from them. She soon learned that the childish old men had spread rumors throughout the village that during her husband's absence she had gotten into a relationship with a young stranger who would enter her house at night, and not come out again until dawn. From the intensity of grief and fury, the young wife tore her robe, and cried more bitterly than she had ever cried in her life. But her husband and her family didn't show her any mercy, and they decided to bring down upon her a severe punishment in defense of their impugned honor. After talking the matter over for a long time, they decided to burn her.

And so it was that they lit a roaring fire near the olive tree that overlooks the spring, where the childish old men used to sit, and they brought her with her arms and legs bound, her head shaved, just like they used to do to two-timing wives. Just as they were about to toss her into the fire, the olive tree barked at them, "Don't treat her like this! She's innocent. Those old men are liars and tyrants!" They immediately retreated, astonished, shocked. The olive tree continued shouting the same thing until they untied her bonds and put out the fire with which they had intended to burn her. And just like that the wife was spared from certain death. As for the childish old men, they received the punishment they deserved as reprimand for slandering her so heinously.

As for me, though, there was neither guardian angel nor sacred olive tree to rescue me from the awful fate that life had in store for me. All alone, with no support or assistance, I continued fighting back against those evil ones who planned one plot after another against me. In the end I was defeated, and they achieved what they had so wanted and yearned for all along!

Now I return to my story to say that fear had been wiped away from me ever since the first day I came out in the finery of a bride ecstatic about her wedding, to stroll through the capital however I pleased. It's true that their spiteful glares and their bawdy comments, their suspicious movements and their mocking laughter, their false rumors and their devilish ruses continued to torment me and burn me up on the inside; on the outside, though, I exerted all of my energy to appear composed and self-confident.

Then I started going out to walk around the capital three or four times a week. My walks got longer. They would begin at ten a.m. and wouldn't end until nearly evening. In that way I managed to get to know many of the famous neighborhoods like Lafayette, where the radio and television building was located, and Montplaisir and al-Umran and Mathildeville, with their embassies and foreign consulates. Strolling through the Belvedere Garden and the Central Market on Charles de Gaulle Street would calm me down even when I didn't buy anything. If I got tired, I'd sit down in one of those swanky cafés in Bab al-Bahr frequented by respectable women to have some coffee or orange juice and read the paper. That's right, I became addicted to reading newspapers, especially *The Dawn*, so I could follow whatever was going on inside and outside the country. In doing that, I felt as though I was a woman of high society, not the wife of a railway worker living in miserable fucking M slum. I won't hide from you the fact that I would grow ever more proud and self-assured whenever men stared long and hard at my body, or let out catcalls as I passed by, or approached me in a nearly deserted street to whisper some words that would melt my heart. I also won't hide from you the fact that some of them invited me to have a drink or to go see a movie, to take a walk in the Belvedere Garden or to take a stroll on the shores of the northern suburbs or in Hammamat, but I didn't accept a single one of their invitations, and I didn't exchange anything more than a few words with those men because what mattered to me most of all wasn't men, but the feeling that I was still beautiful and attractive, and that M Slum hadn't deformed my nature, hadn't wreaked havoc and destruction on my body as it had done with the overwhelming majority of its women.

It was clear that Mansour knew what had been going on while he was away because rage flashed in his eyes like momentary lightning on more than one occasion. Nevertheless, he remained calm and composed, until one night he exploded in anger, shouting in my face, his eyes bulging out of their sockets as he became more repulsive than I'd ever seen him before, "Why have you been going out so much over the past few weeks?!"

I pushed backed at him, angry, and also shouted, "None of your business!"

"How can that be none of my business when I'm your husband?!"

I drew in closer to him. Fixing my eyes on his, with an urge to slap him and knock him to the ground, I yelled, "Do you want me to die of loneliness in this fucking house? Tell me, is that what you want?!"

He hung his head and backed off, confused. He was trembling from head to toe. I don't know if it was out of fear or rage. Then he took refuge in silence, and ran off to bed. As for me, I remained standing there, ready to pounce on him if he dared open his mouth again.

But my life soon took an unexpected turn. . . .

It all happened on one of those days that in our village we call "Wolf's Wedding Day," when the weather alternates between cloudlessness and rain. I was strolling through Bab al-Bahr when I got drenched by a heavy downpour, so I hurried inside the Café Internationale. I ordered a café crème. Just as I was opening up my copy of *The Dawn*, I spotted an elegant woman about my age approaching me with a smile on her face. At first I assumed she was smiling at some woman or man behind me, but she opened her arms wide, ready to embrace me, and shouted, "Have you forgotten me, my dear Najma?" As she took me into her arms, I nearly took flight from joy because she was none other than Maryam, a girl from my village who had left with her family for the capital when she was young and whom I'd only seen once since then, as far as I could remember. Each one of us began sizing up the other, taking stock of what time had done to her.

In her youth, Maryam had been frail, her face had always been filthy, and her skin color tilted toward black. She was agile, combative, insolent, and sharp-tongued, even with those who were much older than she, regardless of whether they were men or women. All of us, men and women alike, would avoid playing games with her because she used to claw at anyone who tried to defy her or insult her or make fun of her, like a wild cat. I remember how I pushed her off of me once with some harshness when we were playing Azim Zara on a moonlit summer night, and she bit my shoulder, leaving visible marks on my skin for several days. Maybe because of all that, we weren't too broken up when she left with her family to move to the capital. But after a few short weeks, we started feeling like she had left behind a gap none of us would be able to fill. And now, here she was in front of me, a woman with a beautiful body, clear-eyed, honey-skinned, with boyish hair, and the elegance of a refined taste. Nothing about her behavior, her movements, or her attire would give the impression that she came from that dirt-poor village. It was as if she were a native of the capital, generation upon generation! With her hands holding mine, she told me, "Believe me, my dear Najma, over the last few weeks, ever since I heard you had gotten married and were living in the capital, I've been thinking about you a lot, but I couldn't find your address. Just now, as I was walking in front of this café, it crossed my mind to come inside. Just like that, out of curiosity; and when I saw you, I felt as though the door of heaven had opened up in front of me. Oh my dear, what an amazing coincidence!"

Still holding my hand, she added, "Do you know you've become even more beautiful?"

"So have you!"

"Ahh, I was never good-looking, but you, ahh . . . you, you were a beauty queen from the moment you dropped out from your mother's belly!" She let out a high-pitched laugh that attracted the attention of a number of other patrons.

Then Maryam recounted some details of her life in extreme brevity. She said she worked in a beauty salon in the Montfleury neighborhood, that she had left home to live with two girlfriends in the same neighborhood where she worked, and that in general she lived a nice life, free of troubles and problems and concerns.

"And are you married?" I asked her.

Maryam scowled just like she used to as a child when she wanted to express disgust with something, and said, "Oh, I don't want to go into all that. Please!"

Again, she held my hand like a sister, and asked me in turn, "What about you?"

My eyes were bathed in tears. I kept silent for a moment, but then pulled myself together. With all the gory details I told her how I had suffered ever since arriving in the capital. When I was finished, I watched sorrow wash over her eyes as if a black cloud were floating across her face.

"And what are you doing now, my dear?" she asked me.

"I'm thinking about getting a divorce!"

"Oh, no. No. Don't even think about it. Please!"

"And why not?"

"Because if you get divorced there'll only be one solution, to go back to the village you managed to escape from. That would be another disaster, don't you think?"

"But what should I do, then?"

"Find yourself a job!"

"A job?"

"That's right. Only a job will let you laugh at your life, as you must."

"But how do I find a job?"

Maryam lowered her head for a moment to think, her left hand on her forehead, and when she lifted her head, the cloud of sorrow shadowing her eyes and face had passed, and she said, "I've got an idea!"

"What?"

"I know this French widow, she's about seventy-five years old. She also lives in Montfleury and is looking for a servant to help take care of her."

Infuriated, I shouted at her, "You want me to become a servant for some European woman?"

She replied immediately with a bit of sharpness, "What's the shame in that?" Then, in a calmer tone, she added, "If you truly want to start your life over again, my dear Najma, you've got to get rid of your village mentality and realize that without money in this dog-eat-dog city you're through, you'll get trampled underfoot without anyone caring one bit. Besides, this French lady is cultured and has virtuous morals. I'm sure she'll treat you like a respectable woman, not a servant."

She was silent for a moment, and then asked me, "Do you want me to give her a call?"

"As you wish . . ."

"We've got to strike while the iron's hot," Maryam said, and then headed for the door. After about ten minutes she came back, her face all cheery. "Let's go," she ordered.

"Where to?"

"To see the French lady. She wants to meet you right away!"

We hopped in a cab and headed for Montfleury. The French lady, whose name was Monique, received us with exaggerated hospitality. She was a petite woman with a small round face, a thin nose, gray eyes, and short henna-colored hair. She was dressed in a blue skirt and a black sweater. She still wore a wedding ring. Despite the exhaustion of old age that was apparent on her face and in how she moved, her face was still defined by some of the radiance of distant youth. Her villa was uniquely well-appointed—carpets from Kairouan, rugs from the south of Tunisia, paintings and photographs, clay ewers and others made from pure copper were set out in front of the sweets and coffee cups scented with rose water. Madame Monique began speaking to us in the dialect of the capital, relying from time to time on words and phrases in French. From what she said, I learned that she was originally from Marseille, and that she had met her husband, a petty officer in the French army, during the Second World War. When she came to Tunisia, she fell in love with the environment and the people. As the days passed, she started to feel Tunisian in spirit and in her heart. She didn't want to leave the country after her husband's death. I also learned that she had two married daughters back home who were both architects, and a married daughter who lived in Paris and was a history professor, and that this daughter, Samia, had invited her on more than one occasion to come and live with her in Paris, but she refused definitively.

"What would I do there? Je vais mourir de tristesse," she said, adding, "Tunisia is very dear to me, very dear. Et Meriem le sait bien, n'est-ce pas Meriem?"

"Oui, madame," Maryam replied.

At that moment Madame Monique asked her, "Quel est le nom de ta copine?"

"Najma, Madame!"

"Oh! Quel joli nom! Et elle est de la région de Kairouan comme toi?"

"Oui, Madame."

"Oh! C'est super! J'aime beaucoup Kairouan. C'est une très belle ville!"

Then Madame Monique turned toward me and asked, "Do you have any children?"

"Non, Madame!"

"Oh! ça me convient très bien!"

We left Madame Monique's place late in the afternoon. The sky was clear, but dark clouds were rapidy approaching from the west. When I hugged Maryam goodbye, I felt that a new chapter in my life had truly begun. The very next day, I started working for Madame Monique.

And Mansour didn't learn about it until an entire month had passed!

THE SON

No doubt you have started to wonder, now that I've told you so many chapters of my life, why I have always persistently avoided talking about my mother. When I have mentioned her, it was only with extreme brevity, and mostly it was about her cunning.

I tell you truthfully that ever since I became conscious of the world around me, my mother had no desire for me to exist at all. That's right, this is how I felt as I took my first steps in life. Why else would my mother have left me almost every day of the week, while I was still crawling, with Umm Maryam, the mother of her friend Maryam, without bringing me back home again until late at night? I won't deny the fact that Umm Maryam, God bless her, was a good-hearted, generous old lady who feared God and loved looking after abandoned children like me. Still, I was in dire need of my mother. I wanted her to touch me, to play with me, to accept me, and to tell me beautiful entertaining stories. But she denied me all of that, on purpose, as far as I could tell. Just like she used to do with my father, she would get as disgusted by me as she was by vile insects, treating me with enmity and harshness, as though I were some other woman's child. Once, when I was three years old, I was home alone with her. Suddenly, there was a clap of thunder and lightning flashed in the sky that had turned black and desolate, like the night in winter. Then a raging storm broke out, and the world started to violently quake. I was petrified and started crying. But my mother kept on cleaning the kitchen without even turning toward me, without paying any attention to me.

When she saw me crying, she attacked me, shouting, with her fist near my head, "Shut up, you son of a bitch, or else. . . ." I swallowed my gasps. From that moment on, for several years, I became fearful of being home alone with her. My fear wouldn't subside until my father came home, my father who loved me more than any other creature in the world. With his every movement, his every glance, and his every word, he used to make me feel like I was his valuable treasure, his hope, his glory, and the symbol of his manhood that my mother would trample upon and insult on a daily basis. From the time I reached the age of four, I began to accompany him on long walks in the markets, through the Belvedere Garden and other places he used to like, which I came to like as well. During the month of Ramadan, he wouldn't deny me a visit to the circus or some special toys. In the summertime, I'd ride the train with him on his weekly day off, and we'd go to the beach at La Marsa or Halq al-Wadi. As for my mother, she never did that with me once, not even once!

After matriculating at school, I started spending summer vacations and some other holidays with my grandmother in the village. Ever since my first visit there, it seemed as though I had found the mother I so desperately needed: the mother who was capable of providing me with unconditional love and tenderness and affection, the mother who wasn't stingy with anything I asked or wished for, the mother who spoiled me rotten, as she should, giving back to me what had been lost and sucked out of my childhood, what I had been deprived of. Therefore I state upon my honor that my maternal grandmother was the greatest and most amazing woman I knew in my short life. She made me forget all about my mother's loathing and her terrible cold silence, especially when we were alone in the house together, so after her death, the gap left by my father's death grew wider and blacker, and my life turned into a series of successive holes; I'd get out of one only to immediately fall into another.

Now, my good people, please allow me to level with you: I was afaid when I first started to mix with the people of the slum because of all the nasty stories that were told about my mother, as if all the other women in the slum were pure, with the exception of her, and her alone. The truth of the matter wasn't so. Everyone in the capital, and maybe outside the capital too, knows full well that M Slum is a hub of corruption and vice and sneakiness and tricks and theft and lying and hypocrisy and every social and psychological disease one can imagine. Everyone also knows that most of its women, married and single, divorced and spinsters and young women who haven't reached the age of eighteen, make a living from secret prostitution, doing it within sight and earshot of their fathers, their husbands, their brothers, and their relatives, as though it was an everyday occurrence. I witnessed this first-hand, especially after I got older and started to frequent the cafés and the hotels in the capital, in the northern suburbs, and elsewhere. I saw with my own eyes a number of mothers and sisters and female relatives of those who used to make my life miserable in school and in the streets and in other places, ripping to shreds my mother's honor in the light of day by claiming they had seen her doing this or that and heard about her doing this or that, sighing in the laps of foreign men in the Ibn Khaldun Hotel and the Diplomat Hotel and the Mashtal Hotel, in Libyan cars on the Corniche with bald pot-bellied men who came from the remote villages and cities of the interior hungry for flesh. That's right, my good people. Nevertheless, I didn't allow myself to talk about those women like the others used to do with my mother. As I already mentioned, I was alarmed at first by the amount of those nasty stories that I used to hear about my mother, but by and by I managed to immunize myself against them. Determined to become a man among men one day, I buried my eyes in courses and books, achieving moderate successes in that way. That's what the good grades I used to get at school demonstrated. But after my father's death, I started to lose my mind and my mother became like an ominous owl as far as I was concerned. Do you know why? Because I sensed, or rather, I became certain that she was the reason for his death. Am I exaggerating? No, my good people, I haven't and will not ever tell a lie because there is no longer anything in my life that can justify my propensity for lying and making false accusations against others, whether they are close to me or far away. Once again I find myself obliged to repeat what I have already mentioned to you on more than one occasion, namely, that my father, may God bless him and install him in the paradise of His heavens, was a peaceable man, his temperament was his own business, as the people in our country would say. He didn't like to mix with people except when he went back to the village, and he wouldn't ever talk about this matter or any other except when he found himself among his family and relatives, and especially with my grandmother who used to treat him as though he were her own son. He used to dislike the people of the capital, calling them "children of the walls." So he used to avoid them, perpetually trying not to run into them because they were all "evil and immoral" in his view (and in mine as well).

He was endowed with rare modesty. I never heard him raise his voice except during that argument when my mother got involved with that scumbag, and he never said a bad word, which was the custom among most men in our country, "proving their vanquished masculinity," as my southern friend Aziz used to explain it. He didn't have a single friend in the neighborhood. I think that was the case for him at work as well because none of his colleagues showed up at his funeral, and we didn't receive a single message of condolence from any of them either. In brief, my father's life, may God remember it fondly, can be summarized as follows: going to work early in the morning, coming home between six and seven in the evening. If he was late, it was for some reason beyond his control. Besides, my father was scrawny. He rejected violence and those who used it or threatened to do so. My mother would have known that all too well. Why else would she have cold-bloodedly pushed him into that battle that was lost before it even began with that son of a bitch, "the prison rat" who had perfected the art of fighting and stabbing with knives, and who all the people of the slum were afraid of, including the other violent criminals? Why? Answer me, my good people. Answer me! As for me, I say to you all, and I am completely confident in myself and in my mental faculties, that she did it because of her absolute certainty that the humiliation that would attach itself to my father on account of that battle would be the reason for his demise. And she was right about that. After my father's death, my relationship with my mother became increasingly troubled and aggravated and just plain bad. We lived under one roof, but we were each living in our own world. There were barriers between us, high walls—actually more like entire continents and vast oceans. We only rarely exchanged any conversation at all. Our discussions were nothing more than abbreviated sentences and cold words from her side, and from mine as well. Avoiding sitting with me or speaking to me, she would disappear for the entire day and wouldn't come home until very late at night, that is, after I would have already finished my chores and started getting ready for bed. Lunches and dinners that I ate in her presence didn't happen more than twice or three times per week, sometimes per month. She wasn't interested in my studies or in my grades the way my father had been, and she didn't ever ask me about them. Never. Whether the food was well cooked or burnt, it was all the same to her. The joy that used to overflow my heart or that would light up my life after every exam and at the end of the school year dried up, just like a dew droplet dries up under

the blazing sun, and when I came home, I no longer heard praise or com-
mendation, not a word of thanks or encouragement; rather, I would find
the house silent, as lifeless as if it had been abandoned for a long time.
Still, I remained diligent about my studies, hopeful to become one of the
best men, who lives in a nice neighborhood, who is seen by the people of
M Slum—who are always hanging out in the streets—in a spiffy car, with
his beautiful, elegant, and respectable wife at his side. But by and by my
resolve started to break apart, until one day I found myself reluctant to
study, unable to do it anymore. When I dropped out, my mother wasn't
sad, didn't despair, didn't even get upset, but rather, simply sufficed with
telling me in her cold voice, always as sharp as a knife, "You have to find a
job as soon as possible!" That's right, my good people, that's what she said
to me, because there was nothing else in the world that mattered to her
except money. Money, money, nothing but money. As for me, her only son,
there was no place for me in her heart or elsewhere. That's what I became
more and more certain of after I informed her how I had made up my
mind to make my way to Italy. The news delighted her like she had never
been delighted before. As her face radiated good news and happiness, she
told me, "If you succeed, you'll secure a future for yourself!" Is it rational,
my good people, for a mother to tell her only son something like that, she
who used to watch on TV those scores of people who had made their way
to Italy or Spain, enduring hunger and cold in death ships or drowning,
only to be devoured by whales in the depths of the sea, or have the surging
waves dump their rotting corpses on the shores? Isn't that incontrovertible proof that my mother would have wished for my demise as quickly as
possible, as she did for my father? So I tossed that match on her body that
had been soaked with gasoline out there in the ravine near the Arches of
Zaghouan with the nonchalance of someone lighting a cigarette, and I
walked away without looking back to cast even a single glance at the
inferno that exploded behind me.

THE MOTHER

In spite of the fact that you are in the world of the living while I'm in the world of the dead, which would make it difficult, that is to say, impossible to imagine the existence of any real connection between us, I can feel how you yearn to hear my commentary, or rather, my commentaries on the matter of the numerous rumors and stories told against me by the people of M Slum. I tell you again that not a single one of those tales reflect even a shred of my personal life, as the imaginations of those people, drowning in vice and corruption and rancor, can't come up with anything except false rumors and lies. It's your right to ask me now: But why were you the only one of the women in M Slum who became a victim of those stories and rumors? That's right, you have every right to ask me such a question. And I'll answer you in absolute honesty and clarity. The first thing I want to say to you is that the women in that miserable filthy slum were so jealous of me that they were willing to do anything that might finally push me out of their sight. As for its men, they all hungered for me. When I shut all the windows in their ugly faces, they were transformed into fierce wolves with no other goal than to do me harm and treat me wrongly, to tarnish my reputation and to pollute my honor. Besides, I was arrogant, self-satisfied, I'd stare back at all of them, men and women, old and young, as though they were nothing but repulsive insects creeping under my feet. That's all there is to it. I'd just add that while it's true I come from a dirt-poor village, my family is honorable, respected, and has virtuous morals. That's what always and eternally made me avoid doing anything that could sully my honor, and diminish its value, and every time I started down the road to hell, my grandmother's angry stern face would be staring at me so I'd jump back, afraid, panicked. It's also true that I hated my husband, that I detested sleeping next to him in the same bed, and I'd avoid walking in the street with him, but I wasn't deceiving him every day the way the people of M Slum used to imagine, and I wasn't just giving my body away for money to anyone who moved or crawled, as they all used to think and as they all used to rumor. What mattered most to me, in fact, was to live my life however I wanted, and to enjoy the pleasures of the world as much as possible, but without getting burned and without that causing me any remorse or pangs of conscience later on. Working for Madame Monique, and later on as an employee in a Gulf embassy after her death, helped to hold the key to my life in my own hand, and not to leave it in the hands of others. The point of working wasn't only to ensure my material independence, but also to guarantee my future, because just a short time after getting married I intuited that Mansour wasn't going to live very long. What I supposed turned out to be true, and so it was that after his passing I didn't find myself in a situation that forced me to madness or suicide, or drowned me in that black despair that continues to slowly incinerate my life until turning it into ashes. In order to be as honest with you as I promised to be from the outset, allow me to say that after I became reacquainted with Maryam, I experienced some facets of life that I had always been yearning for and dreaming of. With her help, I became familiar with a lot of the secrets to living in the capital. In her company I stayed out late and danced the night away in swanky hotels, I attended weddings and amazing, raucous birthday parties. All of that lightened the burden of living in M Slum among people who weren't even able to bear smelling my odor, with a husband I couldn't stand and a son who detested me, possibly even hated me intensely. That's what the heinous act he committed against me proved. I'll tell you about that in a little while.

Maryam is the kind of woman who loves to play with men's hearts. She used to make an art of it. In spite of the fact that men chased after her, she would suffice with having brief, fleeting relationships with them, saying, "I'm like a bird—I hate cages, even if they're gilded!" I won't hide the fact that I relied upon Maryam a great deal, not just because of the lightness of her soul and the sweetness of her tongue and the genuineness of her feelings toward me, but also because she was an expert on the personalities and the attributes of the people in the capital. She saved me from a number of frustrating situations, and she helped me avoid problems that could have brought me difficulties that would have been hard to deal with. In turn, she depended upon me to the point that she couldn't bear to be apart from me, not even for one day. With tears in her eyes, she used to say to me, "I hope, my dear Najma, that I die before you do!" I didn't know what to say to those painful words.

And I won't deny that I loved some men in secret. I think they loved me too, but my relationships with them never went beyond kissing and light touches. I didn't allow any of them to get past that line. But about a year after Mansour's death, I got mixed up in a steamy love story. Here are the details. . . .

It was early autumn. At two in the afternoon I left the Gulf embassy where I was working. I walked toward Pasteur Square with the intention of taking a taxi from there to meet Maryam in Bab al-Bahr. Suddenly, the rain started pouring and the street went dark in front of me, and I could no longer see anything but thick ropes of rain coming down from the sky. I took shelter in the entrance to a building and started looking left and right in the street while I waited for a taxi. That's what I was doing when a fancy car stopped right in front of me and the driver waved for me to get in. I accepted his invitation without any hesistation. He was a fortyish man, as handsome as Omar Sharif in his prime. When he asked me where I was going, I told him, "Bab al-Bahr."

"Me too!" he replied, smiling.

Because of the rain, the traffic on Muhammad V Street was terrible, and most of the cars were honking nearly nonstop, but the driver of the car I was in was apathetically watching the chaos in front of him and behind, to his right and his left, as though he weren't in the thick of it all. Rather, it seemed to me from the look on his face that he was taking pleasure in the curses and insults that were flying through the air. His calm and his conceit attracted me, his apathy and his silent sarcasm mesmerized me, and ambiguous feelings seized my heart as something like the beginnings of a fever spread through my body. When we arrived in Bab al-Bahr, the rain had stopped falling, but thunder continued to crash in the sky that was black with clouds. He stopped the car in front of the Coliseum and, smiling once again, told me, "I think I tackled the assignment as best as I could, wouldn't you say?"

"Thank you very much," I said.

As I was preparing to get out, he asked me, "Don't you want to get together some time?"

"I'd like that very much!" I replied.

He thought for a moment, then said, "The day after tomorrow. Three p.m. Same place. Any objections?"

"No," I said. Then I headed off to see Maryam, my heart singing like a bird that has begun to build its nest in a safe place.

I arrived on time for our rendezvous. He was more handsome and more elegant than the time before. Again he displayed the same calm, the same conceit, the same apathy, the same silent sarcasm. The car transported us toward the northern suburbs as the melodies of foreign dance music made me feel as though I were traveling toward a beautiful world I had never known before, one that resembled the world of the amazing fairy tales of love I used to love to hear when I was younger. At the foot of the Sidi Bou Said Hill, he stopped the car. We leisurely proceeded to climb up the hill, through narrow twisting streets that were nearly deserted. The weather was mild. The air was redolent with the scent of autumn, wet with its early rains, as we gazed out over the turquoise-blue sea. He held my hand and whispered, "You're as beautiful as a Bedouin woman!"

"I am of Bedouin origin," I said.

"What's your name?"

"Najma."

"A name that's become all too rare. It's beautiful. I like it very much," he said, and on his lips there was a smile I could no longer resist the pull of, and then he drew me in close to him. His breaths scalded me and I longed for him to kiss me, and to keep on kissing me until I melted in his arms. But he didn't.

We drank pistachio tea at the High Café, and then returned to the car. On the way back to the capital, he told me his name was Nabil, but he didn't tell me anything else about himself. And I didn't ask because the fire of love had started to burn up my body, causing me to lose my reason, until I no longer knew what I was doing, or what I was saying.

During the following rendezvous, he took me to a small apartment in Montplaisir. It was clear from the simple furniture that he didn't live there, but that it was just a haven where he went from time to time for specific purposes. The autumn rain was tapping against the windows as our naked bodies collided beneath the warm blankets. I closed my eyes and the world shimmered with all the colors of the rainbow!

Over the course of nearly half a year, we continued to rendezvous in the same apartment once or twice a week. Throughout that period, I didn't learn anything more about him than his name and he didn't know anything about me except for mine. Not once did he show even the slightest curiosity to learn about the details of my life, as if my body were enough to extinguish every such desire. In the face of his terrible silence, as vast as an ocean, my burning curiosity when he was away would be extinguished as soon as he drew me in close to his chest, and in my mind all the questions I had wanted to ask him, in order to get inside his life that was shrouded in secrets and ambiguity, and which neither his looks nor his facial features revealed anything about, would evaporate. And so it was that with him I was satisfied with pleasure I had never known the likes of before in my entire life. A pleasure to close my eyes as my body collides with his in order to see the world shimmering with all the colors of the rainbow.

Then, suddenly, he disappeared just as he had appeared in the first place.

We were supposed to meet one Saturday afternoon at three in front of the Municipal Theater, but unusually for him, he didn't show up on time. I waited for a full hour. For nothing! My mind broke into pieces, and until this very moment I don't know how I made it to Maryam's house!

He didn't show up the next day either, or over the next two days. On Thursday, I ran over to the small apartment in Montplaisir. I knocked loudly on the door more than ten times. No answer. On the sixth, seventh, and eighth days it was the same. On the tenth day I looked in the mirror and, just then, saw a different face, one that wasn't my own. A face that had been stripped of life and love, gone sallow, cast upon it the cloud of the final farewell.

And that was how the only love story I had ever known came to an end.

Would you say I'm a sinner, and that I'm not quite as innocent as I've claimed?

Perhaps.

But I was never that woman who the people of M Slum made a hobby out of fabricating lies and false rumors about.

THE SON

That warm summer morning greeted me like a curse or a slap in the face. The news broadcast I heard upon waking up from a long deep sleep in which I was tormented by horrible nightmares contained nothing but tragedies and misfortunes, especially in the Middle East: scores of dead and wounded in the Occupied Territories, kidnapped journalists, terrorist bombings at swanky tourist hotels, children dying every day in Iraq because of the embargo, Saddam Hussein mocking American threats, Syria rejecting Israeli reports that the days of President Hafez al-Asad were numbered, the Taliban forbidding people from listening to music and from wearing white socks, Algerians killing each other in the heart of their capital. It was as though the Arabs were destined to endure torments and sorrows like no other people on earth.

I left the house in a terrible mood. I started walking up Mustafa Khazindar Street as the blazing morning sun scorched the city and the people. Behind me the salt flats of Sijoumi floated in a mirage, and in front of me an unsightly bald man wearing filthy shabby clothes was talking to himself, waving his arms around in extreme agitation, completely unaffected by everything around him. I didn't find this strange because the number of people who had started talking to themselves in our country had increased in a shocking manner over the last few years. This phenomenon puzzled me to no end. In our country there is no civil war as in the case of our neighbors, no terrorist bombings, no tribes, no religious sects, no famine—nothing that can even bring about those sorts of situations.

My friend Aziz told me that this phenomenon could be traced to the fact that the people had lost faith in all forms of media, and even in their nearest and dearest relatives. Therefore they no longer trust anyone but themselves, which is whom they turn to whenever they have to deal with a private or a public problem, so it became normal for us to see people talking to themselves as they walked down the street or strolled through public gardens, as they rode the light rail and other public transportation or sat in front of the piles of folders stacking up on their desks. It may happen that they laugh out loud at something interesting they showed themselves. It also may happen that they get into a fight with themselves just as they would fight with their most bitter enemies. I drew in closer to this man, who seemed to be a creature on the verge of plunging into the void, and I began listening to him. . . .

"The two poems I'll never ever forget in my entire life, I always loved reciting them, I memorized them when I was thirteen, or fourteen, maybe fifteen . . . I forget, too much on my mind makes me forget. . . . Anyway, I was young back then. I loved books and poetry and Egyptian movies and Ismail Yasin and Abdel Salam al-Nabulsi and Nadia Lutfi and Fatin Hamama and Omar Sharif and Hind Rustum and Mahmoud al-Miligi. Some people say they're dead, or are they still alive? Anyway, if they're dead, God bless their souls. If they're still alive, may God grant them long life. Yeah, I was young back then, and I used to sing along with all the neighborhood kids:

Teta Teta Teta / We'll fry it up in oil-ee
As my son pretends to nibble / Then shares it with his brothers
Daddy caught a fish-ee / And hear the skillet sizzle
Nibble with his chompers

"Those melodies are so sweet. I loved them so very, very much. Back then the world was still all right, calm, satisfied, there was none of this stealing, none of this greed, none of this lying, none of this waste, none of the fear of our age. The one who helped me memorize those two poems was very fond of poetry. He studied in the Zaytouna Mosque and he knew al-Mutanabbi and al-Ma'arri and Abu Nuwas and Antar bin Shaddad and Ahmad Shawqi and all those old-timers. We don't have anyone like them today. Ahh. Si al-Sadeq was a great man, God's mercy and blessings be upon him. With him what you saw is what you got, no trickery no devilry, he had a big heart and a generous soul. He had an open hand and such a fluent tongue—I loved to sit beside him every afternoon when his mind was clear. Poetry fell from his mouth like rain, oh my God, but what does the author of those two stanzas say? He says:

I sold him a heart in which he may camp / Inside is the best place for him to sit
His gift worth more than the bindle of the tramp / Maybe t'was right for the penniless to sell it

"Ha, ha, ha, ha, maybe t'was right for the penniless to sell it all right. Si al-Sadeq was right, God's mercy and blessings be upon him. But who can buy me, the penniless man who doesn't even have a franc in his pocket this morning. I don't have anything at all! Let me tell you, not a franc not a flute, even my hair thinned out and my head turned as red as a tomato. Anyone who sees me, they'd say, 'How pitiful that man seems, he has to beg for the Lord's mercy,' from seeing someone who doesn't even have enough to buy a crust of bread. Oh yeah, that's what you've come to, Hamadi, that's what you've come to. And tomorrow your situation's bound to only get worse. That old woman in the neighborhood, Saluha the Horny, who you used to do things to that would drive her out of her mind, she used to curse you every morning, curse you every evening, saying, 'God won't reward you! God won't reward you!' Seems to me her prayer came true, and God heard her, and Hamadi you were a wreck, hungry, naked, despised, humiliated, with no heart to care for you, no house to welcome you, and your wife's your walking catastrophe. She told you she wouldn't be crushed by your fallen state, she'd show you stars in the middle of the day, every day you'd fall into line, the police will come to take you away and everyone will see and laugh at you. Your children won't even speak to you. Your daughter's not even afraid of you. That day she slammed the door in your face and told you, *Get out, crack open a book and educate yourself. You've become a fool and you don't even know it!* God, God . . . ahh Hamadi, oh my brother. How time has turned on you. You used to wander and your pocket was always full and the people would hold you in esteem and respect you and fear you. Not a single person could cross the line with you, but today. Ahhh, today, what a disgrace!

The time of connection came and went / Somebody shouted, come on let's cry out our eyes
Can't you see that the papers held a mourning / And now he's burdened with tears

"May God have mercy on the one who uttered those two stanzas. May God have mercy on him. May God have mercy on him!"

At this point the man fell silent and continued making his way up the street that ends in the shape of a camel's neck. His forehead was dripping with sweat. He was exhausted and extremely agitated. When he reached 9 April Street, he stopped walking and began looking in panic at the active traffic at the intersection. Just then, he started slapping his face and violently pounding on his chest, shouting, "Save me, people! Save me! Save me!" But the people continued on their way, uninterested in him. When he grew tired of slapping and beating and shouting, he collapsed on the pavement, blue in the face, white-eyed. At that moment he was surrounded by pedestrians. As for me, I had moved away from him, trembling from head to toe for some reason I couldn't divine. Maybe I assumed that I would wind up just like him one day. Raving in the street, and continuing to rave and rave until I fall down destroyed.

Once I passed through al-Qasaba Square and took my first steps into al-Aswaq, I felt something sprout out of my behind, something like a tail. I looked behind me in terror and people were staring at my lower half. Some were staring in utter amazement and some were making fun of me, cursing. They soon started laughing out loud, clapping their hands together, or pointing at my lower half. *A tail! A tail! It's definitely a tail!* I thought to myself, swirling my tongue around in my mouth, all my saliva completely dried up. The laughter proceeded to swell louder and louder until I could no longer see anything but the mouths of those people, as black as caves. I ran away and found myself in a narrow alleyway that was completely empty. I leaned my back up against the wall that reeked of piss and garbage that had piled up for days on end and touched my behind. At that moment I felt a rough tail, covered with thick hair. *Oh God! Oh God! What have I done to be afflicted with this curse?* I continued touching my behind: *A tail! A tail!* I bent over and looked between my legs and saw it dangling there, repulsive, horrible. I stood up straight. My body broke out in a cold sweat, as cold as winter ice. I shut my eyes, wishing for the earth to open up and swallow me at once. Then a window high on the wall opposite me opened up and an old gray-haired woman leaned out and shouted at me, "What are you doing down there, you son of a bitch?"

I ran away without responding. Before reaching the street that was still jammed with people I touched my behind one more time and, just then, the tail disappeared. But had it really? I touched my behind a second time, then a third and a fourth. There was no trace of it! I breathed a sigh of relief. The icy sweat that had been drenching my body quickly dried, I regained my composure, and my heart rate stabilized. I mixed in with the people as they went about their business. None of them bothered to even look at me. The tail must have disappeared! But how had it ever appeared in the first place, and how had it disappeared so suddenly? I was still puzzling over that question when, passing by in front of the Zaytouna Mosque, I sensed that my head was no longer my own but something else instead, as if it were the head of one of those miserable donkeys I always used to see wandering in the fields out there in my grandmother's village or straining beneath an unbearable burden or tied up in the shade on blazing-hot days, its eyes closed, enjoying the break it rarely received after the hard labor it was subjected to on a daily basis. When I glanced in the mirror at some shop I passed by, where my head should have been I saw the head of a donkey with scandalously floppy ears, and in my eyes a misery I'd never seen the likes of before, neither in the eyes of an animal nor those of a human being. I ran through the narrow, interconnected streets as laughter pursued me like painful lashings. I cut through Bab al-Jadidi, then Bab Aliwa, then the al-Jalaz Cemetery and then al-Muruj. I ran without stopping. I ran and ran and ran. I ran away from the city that had become a terrifying ogre, from the mocking and cursing laughter, from the black nightmares that had started tormenting me at night and during the day and from the people of M Slum, from their lies, their false rumors, and the poison of their deadly resentments, from everything in my life that was no longer tolerable. When I no longer had the strength to keep running, I stopped, wheezing. My breathing nearly stopped. The Arches of Zaghouan were to my right and all around me the bare earth was moaning beneath the heat of summer. In front of me there was a black ravine that I had seen in a few of my nightmares.

I touched my head.

The donkey's head had disappeared.

THE MOTHER

No, no, no. I never wanted to be a mother, not to a girl, not to a boy, but fate had me in its sights. What could I do? The first thing I want to say to you on this topic is that I never imagined that letting Mansour's revolting snake near my body from time to time could have any effect, so I thought nothing of the matter and I remained oblivious until my stomach started to expand. At that point, I gave the matter up to God. And so it was that after two years of being married, while I was home visiting the village, I gave birth to a son. My mother was delighted and she chose for him the name of a hero from one of her many fairy tales. In Mansour's face, which was always inscrutable, revealing no sorrow or joy or any other feelings, I saw an amazing light that just might have been the light of happiness, illuminating him now that he had successfuly demonstrated his manhood to all the people of the village.

I'll confess that my son disliked me from the very beginning. That's right, from the very beginning. That is, before he even knew how to walk and talk. I wonder, as he was dropping out of my belly, could he sense that I never wanted him to come into the world? That's certainly possible. The first four years of his life nearly drove me insane, or to something that was no better. Whenever we were alone in the house together, just him and me, he'd start to cry, carrying on like that for hours and hours, until I was overcome with the desire to strangle him or smash his head against the wall, or else abandon him there all alone and run far, far away! Far, far away! Somewhere at the end of the earth. Ahh, how he would cry!

And how sad and forlorn his crying was! I was incapable of shutting him up. And he'd just keep on crying and crying and crying, until the world with all its water and vegetation and people and everyone who has any connection to life comes to an end, becoming a desert with no beginning and no end. I don't think there's ever been a baby in the whole wide world who could cry like my son, not even those children in catastrophes and disasters that we saw on television! As the days passed, his crying would get buried like a knife in my soul, in my body, following me everywhere I went. Even when I was asleep, I would hear him. Crying. Crying. Crying. Without a rest. The amazing thing is that he would calm down completely whenever he was with his father, or whenever he was at Umm Maryam's, with whom I used to leave him while I was at work, or when I went out with Maryam.

When he turned four, he stopped crying once and for all, but his dislike of me remained concealed inside him, like a fire smoldering under ashes. Whenever we were alone, I'd steal a glance at him and catch him staring at me with suspicion and caution and anxiety. As if he were afraid I might harm him! But whenever his father was around, he'd become a different child, a child who laughs and plays, quick-tongued, bright-faced, calm, even-keeled, as nimble as a delighted bird in springtime. His behavior invigorated Mansour, spreading through him happiness and joy and the pride of fatherhood, until his droopy sorrowful face would radiate the same brilliance I had seen the day his son was born. I became even more infuriated and my soul was poisoned with the bitterness of alienation, the alienation of a mother who lives with a husband she doesn't love and a son who is both afraid of her and detests her!

At school he showed an aptitude I never would have expected from him, he got good grades, and Mansour became increasingly infatuated with him and proud of him, proceeding to spoil him more than necessary most of the time, attending to him the way a gardener cares for a flower he is afraid will wilt and die before its time. On holidays, Mansour would make sure to take him to the village and show him off in front of the people there. Where his family line had once been threatened with extinction, he now had an heir. On one occasion I heard him tell his mother, "Alaa al-Din is the most beautiful and most precious gift from God. I'm sure he's going to grow up to be an important person one day!"

My mother doted on him, and he hung on her as well, so he started going back to visit the village for every vacation, even on harvests and holidays. Whenever he didn't come, she'd send protest after protest. It was clear that she wasn't just a grandmother to him, but a mother too. That's something I witnessed with my own two eyes. She wouldn't hesitate to expound, around me or anyone else, how Alaa al-Din was the best of all her grandchildren, the best tempered and the most intelligent. She would burst out crying whenever she saw him coming and she'd do the same thing when she had to hug him goodbye. After returning from the village, he wouldn't talk about anything else but her. Just about her. As if he hadn't seen anyone else but her and her alone!

He memorized some of her stories and tales by heart. On weekend nights, he would tell them to his breathless father in his pleasant voice, and with his extraordinary memory that was like the popular storytellers in our village. I would watch all of this as it happened, frozen in place, confused, silent, unable to redirect the flow of the river that was moving farther and farther away from me day after day. The boy refused to do anything that might help me break down the wall of disgust he had built up between the two us ever since he started creeping along the face of the earth. He would do everything in his power to keep me distant, removed. As if he hadn't spent nine months in my womb! What happened next caused the wall of disgust between him and me to rise up even higher and become more solid still. Here are the details. . . .

I already told you how from the moment I arrived in M Slum all the men there—married and unmarried alike—wouldn't stop harassing me, using the nastiest and most despicable means to do so. That ugly-faced son of a bitch, his appearance deformed with gashes and battle scars, who had spent more time in prison than out of it, was the most aggressive of them all, the fiercest toward me. The last time he got out of prison, after spending a year on the inside, as far as I know, he started to get in my way in the morning and at night, whispering silly and vile words of flirtation that would splatter my soul and my body with asphalt and tar. When he got fed up with my resistance, he would begin to threaten me, saying that he was going to disgrace me in front of the entire slum, and that he was going to divulge to the people all the secrets of my life that nobody but he knew about. He persisted in annoying and threatening me for days upon weeks while I was patient, silent, exerting all of my energy to hold myself together and remain calm, until one evening, as I was coming home after work, and the street was empty and dark, he jumped out in front of me baring his ugly teeth and flashing me, whispering as he stroked his erect thing, "Look at it. Don't you like that? Take a long hard look. It's awesome, isn't it? You won't find anything like it in all of Tunisia. Look! Don't you like it? Don't you like it?" Then he let out a long laugh.

I raced inside the house in a state of nausea. I collapsed on the couch in the living room, with a bitter taste in my mouth. My head was spinning, my heartbeat was weak, on the verge of stopping altogether. I looked over at Mansour. As usual, he was sitting there in front of the television, calm, silent, uninterested in my presence. His head was buried between his shoulders like all pathetic submissive men. His son sat beside him, taking on his appearance, as though he were a smaller version of him. A storm of black rage overwhelmed me and I shouted at Mansour, demanding that he do something, anything, to drive away that son of a bitch who had started to make my life miserable on a daily basis, and he became even more withdrawn, more frail. My anger grew sharper, and I uttered some things that must have cut him deep, because he kept on groaning in pain the whole night through, whimpering like a wounded animal.

The truth of the matter is that I had known that Mansour wouldn't be able to confront that son of a bitch who was feared by everyone in the slum, including the most hardened criminals, because what can a small pathetic animal do in the face of a beast of prey? Still, I had hoped to see Mansour, if only just once, give up the repulsive form that had enveloped him, which he no longer even tried to leave . . . the form of a submissive, pathetic, cowardly, peaceable, silent, tranquil, frozen, obliterated, over-whelmed, obscure, beaten-down man. I used to want to see him upset, exasperated with me and with himself, the people, the entire world, and to hear him cry out and shout and protest and swear and curse people and threaten and vow to do something like 'passionate' men do. That's right . . . this is what I used to want and hope for . . . but the next morning, when I saw him heading toward that evil son of a bitch's house, hell-bent on chewing him out, I was certain I had made a big mistake that there was no way I would be able to fix.

I shut my eyes, I covered my ears, and I waited.

When Mansour came staggering in, dripping with blood and mud, I suspected that his death was drawing near, and he confirmed my intuition because after a few months had passed, Mansour spit up blood one morning at dawn and we took him to the Charles Nicole Hospital in a coma-like state. The next evening, his soul went up to his Creator.

That was God's will, my good people. But after that incident my son started treating me as if I were his father's murderer, and he only rarely ever spoke to me. When he did, he usually had a frown on his face, all agitated in his movements and his speech. He refused to show me his grades like he used to do with his father. He wouldn't eat at the same table with me. He wouldn't smile at me on joyous days or congratulate me from afar. He wouldn't show me friendship of any kind. In brief, he was treating me like his mortal enemy. On holidays, he'd go to the village and search at my mother's for what might compensate for the gap left behind by his father.

After my mother died, my relationship with him got really bad. He was sixteen years old at the time. One day, I'm not exactly sure what I said or did, he started smashing plates and glasses, and swearing, shouting and threatening to burn the house down. Horror froze me, and I just stood there, unable to do anything. He was smashing things, making threats, and cursing, shouting like a lunatic. From that moment on, these fits of rage started overcoming him at least once a week.

Then he dropped out of school in spite of the fact that he got good grades. When I tried to ask him why, he foamed at the mouth and shouted back at me, his eyes inflamed with malice and anger. "That's my business!" he snarled. "And from now on I don't want you meddling in my affairs!" I started to become afraid of him, afraid of his threats, so I complained to Maryam about it. After listening to me for a long time, she said, "My dear Najma, you should just leave him alone. Maybe God will resolve his situation someday."

I followed her advice and left him alone.

THE SON

I was in a garden that may very well have been the Belvedere Garden in the capital, except for the fact that it was devoid of people and had the desolation of winter. I had been crying silently, with my head buried between my arms. Just then, suddenly, from behind the mist of my steadily falling tears, I saw a specter approaching. The specter gradually started growing clearer and clearer until it turned into my father. I jumped up and ran toward him. He embraced me warmly, just like he used to do when I was a little boy, held my hand and whispered, "Come along, my dear boy. Come along now!"

I wanted to ask him where we were headed but he raised his right index finger to his lips, indicating for me to keep quiet. I can't say for certain how long we walked. The streets were empty. No cars. No people. Then there rose up in front of us an enormous hotel with a façade that was adorned with the flags of Arab and European countries, and standing to the right and the left of its wide glass door there were severe boorish guards dressed in red uniforms, wearing red hats, too. They glared at us with scorn and contempt. The older one shouted at us, "You're not allowed inside. Come on, get out of here or I'll call the cops!" My father didn't protest, he just gently squeezed my hand and whispered, "Don't worry. We'll find another way to get in despite them!"

We walked away from the front door and headed around toward the rear entrance. It was wide open. There were no guards. First we walked through a dim hallway, until we entered a small glass room that overlooked a spacious ballroom teeming with patrons: men and woman of all ages and races, Arabs and Europeans, maybe even Asians as well. They were talking and drinking in an atmosphere of concord and affection and glee. At this point distinctive Oriental music was struck up. From behind the white silk curtain, my mother appeared, dressed in shameless attire that showed off her feminine charms, and she started to dance, shaking her buttocks and her breasts in a lewd manner, like the female dancers in Egyptian movies. I turned my head away disapprovingly, and my father shook me violently, whispering, this time in an infuriated tone, "No. No. Don't look away. You've got to know what your mother does on the sly. You've got to know!"

I obeyed him, and continued to watch what was happening in that spacious ballroom. My mother carried on with her lewd dance, sending out smiles to everyone in the crowd. The patrons were clapping and shouting out expressions of wonderment and praise. Some of them even approached her and smashed bills between her breasts, or around her waist! As she danced and danced and danced I glanced over at my father and, just then, he broke out in bitter tears. Afterward, wiping away his tears, he whispered to me in a trembling, choked voice, "Now do you see what your mother does, Alaa al-Din?"

I nodded my head in the affirmative, and he held my hand as we walked out of the glass room, the Oriental music and the shouts of wonderment and praise receding behind us. We walked through the empty streets. When I looked up we were at the edge of the village cemetery. My father stopped. He pulled me in close to his chest and cried. I closed my eyes that were all wet with tears and I longed to stay there in his arms for a long time. When I opened my eyes, there was no trace of him. . . .

That's the dream I had just one week before the event.

THE MOTHER

The trap had been set with precision, and I fell into its snares so easily!

A few weeks before the monstrous act, my son turned into an angel overnight. That's right my good people, he became like a merciful angel with me, smiling in my face as I was leaving the house or coming home, treating me kindly, telling me sweet things when I got home from work exhausted, making my morning coffee and helping me clean the kitchen; he even apologized on more than one occasion for ugly things he may have done to me in the past, asking for pardon and forgiveness. His behavior puzzled me at first, but when I recalled what Maryam had said to me on the day I complained to her about his severity and his aggressiveness toward me, my puzzlement dissipated, and I thought that God had finally resolved his situation, that in the future he wouldn't dare to violate the sanctity of motherhood, that he wouldn't let the rumors of M Slum get to him, and that he wouldn't treat me as though I were his mortal enemy, as he had in the past. Instead, I was delighted with the unexpected transformations, and Maryam told me, "Listen, my dear Najma, the best thing you can do is to turn the page on the past and be optimistic about the future. Now you have a son who is capable of protecting you from the evil of those bastards in the slum where you live."

Then my son started telling me about a friend of his named Aziz. He told me that he was a friendly and considerate young man, and that he was going to help him get his hands on a passport because his uncle was a senior representative in the Ministry of Interior.

"But why do you need a passport?" I asked him.

"Because I want to travel abroad."

"And go where?"

"Italy."

"But why Italy?"

"Aziz's brother has been living there for the past six years and he promised to help get me a job in the restaurant where he's head chef."

He was silent for a moment, before adding, "I don't want to 'burn' my way like everyone else does. That's a very dangerous thing to do. I want to go abroad in a legal manner. Aziz's brother swears he'll do whatever he can so I can go to Italy with him at the end of the summer."

He became distracted for a brief moment, and then, as his eyes shone with joy and hope, he said, "My heart tells me I can make a lot of money in Italy. Then I'll be able to buy a house far away from this filthy slum!"

As I listened to what he was saying, the horizon opened up before me so I could see myself as a respectable woman reclining on a couch on a balcony in a house overlooking the sea. I closed my eyes, taking pleasure in the marvelous dream, and then told my son, "May God help you, my son. Do whatever it is that you desire. I'm with you and my heart is with you!"

Three days before the event, my son barged in on me as I was getting ready to go to sleep, saying, "I want to ask you for something and I hope you won't say no!"

"What is it?"

"Aziz's brother, the one I told you about, is getting married next Sunday. The wedding's going to be in their family village near the Arches of Zaghouan, and you're invited!"

I agreed without any hesitation!

On Sunday, at three p.m., we took a taxi to the Arches of Zaghouan. The heat was brutal, the cicadas were chirping, and the world was swimming in a mirage. My son pointed toward a small rise and said, "The village is just over that hill!"

We walked across the empty, desolate fields. After we had walked for several hundred meters, I started panting, my clothes were spotting with sweat, the dust was disguising my shoes, and I could feel that my make-up had smeared. I was about to express my annoyance about the heat and the dust to my son, when I received a powerful blow on the back of my head and blacked out.

When I regained consciousness, I was down in a ravine, my mouth was gagged, and my hands and legs were bound. My son was pouring gasoline all over my body. Then, in absolute calm, he tossed a lit match and scrambled out of the ravine, sure-footed, without looking back. As the fire raged, I felt as though it wasn't just going to consume my body but the entire world along with it. . . .

THE SON

My grandmother named me after the hero of her favorite fairy tale, by which I mean Alaa al-Din in the Land of Terrors, perhaps thinking that it would be possible for me to prevail over the traps of the world as he had. But she was wrong. For the heroes of fairy tales are always and eternally luckier than people like me, who are destined to live a miserable life in a miserable reality. Besides, fate always and eternally grants the heroes of fairy tales the chance for salvation or victory, even in those moments when we're certain that their end or their loss is undoubted and indisputable. As for my kind, ahhh, well, fate usually has those of my kind in its sights. Still, I love the story of Alaa al-Din, and so, before I bid you the final farewell, I have made up my mind to tell you the remaining chapters of the fairy tale. And I say to you: come one come all, hear ye hear ye, God guides us and guides you to see. When we last left Alaa al-Din, he was trying to solve the riddle of the locked room, not knowing that Princess Shayma was locked up inside. One evening, while he was sitting in front of the door thinking about its secret, a bird as beautiful as a peacock flew over top of him, dropping a piece of paper in his lap and disappearing out of sight. Alaa al-Din picked up the piece of paper, unfolded it, and saw that it was a letter from the King of Light informing him of Princess Shayma's situation, asking him to memorize the following phrase by heart: "Hash adja tneekso tukreeho laka yaff halla dahaw hana yala ladat yata hal yash laka yaqu." If he stuttered in pronouncing it, even only once, then the locked room wouldn't open. He had to repeat the very same line in order to open the large fortress gate. Once outside the gate, he'd find a horse that would transport him and Princess Shayma at the speed of the wind to the Valley of the Snakes. From that point on, the two of them would be on their own. The King of Light mentioned that he would distract the King of Shadows with wars and conflicts so that he wouldn't be able to follow Alaa al-Din and Princess Shayma. Finally, the King of Light advised Alaa al-Din to be careful during his long journey toward his father's country, throughout which he would be confronted with dangers and many terrors.

If they managed to survive them all, the King of Shadows would be forced to acquiesce to the status quo, following the rules that he must not pursue anyone who manages to escape from his clutches.

Alaa al-Din spent the night repeating that strange phrase until he had memorized it by heart as the King of Light had advised him to do. When he pronounced it correctly in front of the locked room, the door opened, and Princess Shayma appeared, pale-faced and sad. Alaa al-Din introduced himself and told her all about what had happened to him with the King of Shadows, and her face regained its radiance and its freshness, and she told him, smiling, "While I was locked up in that room, I dreamed that someone who looks just like you would come and rescue me!" At the main fortress gate, Alaa al-Din repeated the strange phrase and it opened, and a horse appeared right there in front of him, as if it were made of light. Alaa al-Din seated Princess Shayma behind him and the horse shot off with the two of them at the speed of the wind. Before night fell, they had reached the Valley of the Snakes. As soon as they dismounted, the horse disappeared.

This Valley of the Snakes was vast, desolate, overgrown with thorns, and teeming with so many serpents writhing around one another that neither one of them could touch the ground. Staring at the staggering number of serpents, Alaa al-Din was scared, and wondered to himself, "If the first obstacle is this hard, what are the other obstacles we're about to face on our long journey going to be like?"

Princess Shayma started shaking from the intensity of her panic, and she was gripped with the feeling that it would be impossible to continue their journey.

As night fell, the two of them saw a fire and headed toward it, and, just then, they came upon on old wisewoman sitting outside a straw hut and eating some dry bread. They greeted her and she responded pleasantly, telling both of them, "I'd be so happy if you would share this dry crust of bread with me, because it's all I have to offer!"

They both thanked her for it, then they told her their stories, and she advised them, "You shouldn't stay here too long. As for the snakes, I know they love to hear singing just before sunrise. If one of you is any good, you'll be able to pass through the valley safely!"

Princess Shayma had had a pleasant voice ever since she was a little girl. She had memorized a lot of songs. When she sang, the old wisewoman called out *"la ilaha illa Allah* and *Allahu akbar,"* before shouting, "What an angelic voice, my child. I'm sure the snakes will dance with joy when they hear it. Don't worry about a thing!"

At dawn, Alaa al-Din and Shayma said goodbye to the old wisewoman and headed toward the valley. As they drew closer, Shayma raised her voice up in song and, just then, the serpents pulled away from one another and started to dance, clearing a path in front of her and Alaa al-Din. Once out of the Valley of the Snakes, Alaa al-Din and Princess Shayma walked across thorny, craggy terrain for three days. During the midmorning of the fourth day, Shayma grew so hungry and thirsty and worn-out that Alaa al-Din was forced to carry her on his back. One hour later, two black mountains rose up in front of them, separated by a narrow path. There were many fruitful trees and natural springs so they ate and drank and washed up, and then sprawled out beneath a tree with abundant shade and fell into a deep sleep. When they awoke, the sun was about to set, and the weather had grown cold. They started a fire and they began to tell each other their life's secrets. They were still doing that when a scruffy-bearded, dusty-faced old man dressed in wool appeared in front of them, startling Princess Shayma. Alaa al-Din, for his part, stood up, ready for a fight. But the old man, who still retained great physical strength and agility, just smiled and said to them, "Don't be afraid. I've lived here for almost fifty years and in all those years I haven't harmed a soul who passed through. On the contrary, I've always tried to extend my hand in assistance to anyone who needed it!"

Then the old man sat down in front of the fire, and after listening to each of their stories, he said, "When you two arrived here, you must have seen a narrow path between the two black mountains?"

"Yes, we saw it," replied Alaa al-Din.

"That path is kind of strange. You see, it gets so cold at night that after walking just a few hundred meters on it you freeze, but during the daytime, it gets so hot that anyone who walks on it will burn up after crossing the same distance!"

"So, it's not possible to walk on it then," Alaa al-Din said.

"That's right. Most who try are either frozen or incinerated. But there is one way of getting past."

"What is it?" Alaa al-Din asked.

"At the partition between night and day, the path becomes normal. It's neither cold nor hot. The only danger then is that the path is long, so if you don't make it to the end during that brief period of time, you'll die by incineration. "

Alaa al-Din thought for a bit, then he looked at Princess Shayma, who he found as fresh as a rose greeting a sunny morning. There wasn't a hint of exhaustion on her face from their arduous four-day journey. At that moment he turned to the old man and said, "With God's help I think we'll be able to walk the path!"

The old man smiled again, and, with the light of wisdom in his eyes, said, "I also believe you'll be able to do it. Beyond this path, you'll face other obstacles that might be even more difficult. But have no fear, ancient wisdom says there isn't a human being on the face of the earth whose road will not run into obstacles such as these, but the entire path, until its very end, will be revealed to whoever vanquishes every one of those obstacles. On the other hand, the path will continue on endlessly in front of anyone who remains standing behind every obstacle!"

As the white thread partitioning night from day gradually appeared, Alaa al-Din and Princess Shayma set off toward the path. After taking their first steps, they felt as though an awesome force was pushing them forward, until they felt like they were flying across the face of the earth. And so it was that they managed to reach the end of the path just before sunrise; they breathed a sigh of relief and thanked God for their safe arrival, before continuing on their journey through dense forests with many brooks and astonishing birds they had never seen before. On the fifth day, they sighted a big city on a river in the distance, and they headed toward it, but as they were approaching the city, men wearing animal pelts, with pierced ears and beards and long hair came out of the copse and captured them, shouting and barking like dogs, speaking an incomprehensible language, brandishing swords and daggers and other weapons.

In the city, Alaa al-Din and Princess Shayma noticed that everyone looked like those men who had captured them. They were shouting and barking like dogs nonstop just like them. The women were all wearing animal skins, too; hideous, they had the same voices, movements, and severity as the men. Some of the women looked at Princess Shayma with disgust and contempt, spitting on the ground as they wrinkled their foreheads.

In the middle of the city, along the length of a broad plaza, there were large metal cages. All of them were empty, except for two: in one there was a young man who looked exhausted, haggard, and scared; in the second there was a middle-aged man of about fifty years old who was calm, apathetic.

After they locked Alaa al-Din in one cage and Princess Shayma in a neighboring cage, those boorish men started addresssing the two of them in their incomprehensible language. Soon the middle-aged man rushed to intervene, saying that he could understand this people's language, and that they were telling the two of them how the law forbade foreigners from entering the city, so they had locked them both up to await trial. After the men had gone, the middle-aged man let out a long sigh and said, "You know, O attractive young lady and handsome young man, that the two of you are now in 'Noise City,' possibly so named because its people never stop shouting and barking like dogs, even at night. They intensely despise foreigners. At the end of every month, the city is attacked by an enormous dragon, which lays waste to their livestock and destroys their homes, especially those along the riverbanks. To try to appease it, they started offering up whatever foreigners they capture; all those new cages you see here were once filled with them, but the people of this city offered them to the dragon without batting an eye. This pathetic young man here lost his power of speech from the terror of what he has seen and heard. As for me, I say sadness is no longer necessary in life!"

The middle-aged man was silent for a moment, and then added, "I think the dragon will attack the city in two days, three at most—and the four of us are going to be his meal!"

Alaa al-Din crumpled up in a heap in one corner of his cage, then whispered to himself with his eyes shut, "It's impossible to get past this obstacle. There's no other way out for us than to accept what has been written for us!" Princess Shayma burst out crying, cursing the bad luck that had forced itself upon her, to have to live through misfortunes and tragedies while she was still in the prime of her youth. Night fell. The aging night guard came around to serve dinner to the four detainees. When he had finished, he kneeled in front of Princess Shayma's cage and started staring at her, aghast, his mouth agape, spittle dripping down his filthy beard. He remained like that for two hours, or possibly even more, until sleep overcame him and his snoring rose up loudly. Alaa al-Din watched him when, just then, the guard's keys dropped onto the ground, near the cage of Princess Shayma, who quickly realized this from his gestures, so she reached out her hand, and with the greatest of ease, pulled the keys toward her. After opening her own cage, she unlocked the cages of the other three prisoners. And they all slipped away, fleeing that hideous city.

After walking for two weeks straight through the rugged woods and the dense forests, the four travelers arrived in a land called Ramni, a land of many wonders, where there were abundant ebony trees and rubies and gold; when they entered its capital, an extraordinary city on the sea, they found its markets flourishing, its streets clean, and its citizens living a life of luxury and opulence. Alaa al-Din and Princess Shayma believed they had finally reached Shangri-la, and that they wouldn't have to face any more dangers in the future. But what the two of them didn't know was that the king of that land was a hedonist, a lover of women, especially virgins. Therefore he would send his scouts out in every direction, even up into the mountains and out to the distant countrysides, to search for them. When his spies saw Princess Shayma wandering though the city markets, accompanied by Alaa al-Din, the middle-aged man, and the young man who had regained his power of speech after being freed from the metal cage in 'Noise City,' they ran back to inform the king. Upon hearing of of her, the king ordered them to bring her to him at once. The four travelers were eating dinner at a restaurant on the sea when armed guards surrounded them. Their leader approached Princess Shayma and, after bowing before her, kindly informed her, "My lady . . . Our dear ruler, May God grant him long life and guide his way, desires to have an audience with you in his palace at once!"

When Princess Shayma refused the royal invitation, the leader of the guards got upset and started threatening her, in a subtle manner at first, and more clearly as time went by. At that moment, Alaa al-Din flew off the handle, shouting at the leader of the royal guards, "Listen up, you tell your king that Princess Shayma comes from a respectable family, and as a guest in your land, she demands to be treated according to the convention of her pedigree and her status!"

When the guards transmitted what both Princess Shayma and Alaa al-Din had said, the king of Ramni nearly lost his mind, and he ordered both of them to be brought immediately. As Princess Shayma stood there before him, the king reclined on a comfortable bed adorned with gilded decorations, with meat and fish and fruit and many beverages laid out in front of him, and there was a bevy of blondes and olive-skinned women and Africans all around him, his face stricken with astonishment. For a few moments, he continued to stare at her enchanting face and slender body. Then he kindly said, "O, dear princess, why have you refused my invitation?"

"I thank you very much for your gracious invitation, Your Highness, but it is hard for me to be apart from my betrothed, even if only for a single moment."

And as you all know—come one come all, hear ye hear ye, God guides us and guides you to see—Princess Shayma was not betrothed to Alaa al-Din, but she pretended to be, thinking that the king would take the matter into consideration, because the morals she was raised with and had grown up around dictate that honorable men would never get near pious women. But the king of Ramni had the attributes of scoundrels who enjoy kidnapping women from their husbands by force! So the look on his face changed and he shouted, "And who is this betrothed of whom you speak?"

When Princess Shayma pointed to Alaa al-Din, the king's rage grew even more intense, and, staring at him with contempt, he shouted a second time, "And how is it that such a beautiful princess would accept this pathetic little boy as her betrothed?"

Now, at this point, Alaa al-Din could no longer put up with this, and he thundered, "O King, I hold you in high regard and esteem, but I will not permit you, or anyone else, to besmirch my honor!"

Without saying a word, the king of Ramni gestured toward his guards, who set upon Alaa al-Din and marched him out of the royal court in handcuffs. That very same night, he issued his decree punishing Alaa al-Din in the same manner he punished all opponents of his rule: he would be sprayed in the face with a liquid substance that would blind him; then thrown into the forest, to be eaten by wild animals or else die of thirst and hunger!

The next morning, Alaa al-Din was dumped at the edge of the forest, and he was blind!

Darkness. Silence. Hunger. Thirst.

Alaa al-Din didn't know how much time had passed in which he suffered like that before a bird started to sing, and he was delighted because birds typically only sing where there is water and vegetation.

Feeling his way through the never-ending darkness, Alaa al-Din stumbled in the direction of the bird's voice until he heard the sound of rushing water. He became even more spirited and continued walking. With each step, the sound of rushing water became clearer. Just then, his right foot was soaked with cold water, and he thanked God!

He drank and washed himself, and when he was done, he heard a voice whisper to him, "I'm the sacred tree, and I'm very close to you right now. Chew up some of my leaves, place them over your eyes, and you shall regain your sight!"

He took a few steps forward, until he felt he was in the shade of a tree. He raised his hands and plucked off a few leaves. He chewed them up, placed them over his eyes, and layed down on the cold invigorating earth. After about an hour, the darkness was peeled away and the glorious light shined in! And Alaa al-Din thanked God once again.

Disguised in beggar's clothing, Alaa al-Din returned to the capital of the Kingdom of Ramni and began walking through the streets, the markets and the gardens, eavesdropping on people's conversations, trying to gather some information about Princess Shayma or about anyone else that could help him find her, but the people of that kingdom were nervous about getting involved in the affairs of their king for fear of being persecuted. What's more, the life of luxury to which they were accustomed prevented them from doing so. And so it was that Alaa al-Din spent three days without any information about Princess Shayma. Then one night, in order to get some sleep he took shelter in a ruin on the edge of the city, where he heard an old man ask his elderly wife, "So what about Princess Shayma. Is she still refusing the king's proposal?"

"Yes, the poor girl," his wife replied. "Ever since the king locked her up in his palace she won't eat, won't sleep. She's always crying, so much that she's now as dry as a twig. But the king still desires her, and he keeps on ordering us to do everything in our power to make her give in to him, but I think she'd rather die before giving him what he's after!"

"Anything's possible, of course," the old man commented, "but forcing a woman to love a man she doesn't desire, now that's impossible!"

Alaa al-Din's soul cracked like dry earth after rain. Without any hesitation, he knocked on the door of the elderly couple, and the wife opened the door for him. He asked her if he could come inside, and she allowed him do so. He told the old woman and her husband what had happened to him and Princess Shayma, and she said, "Listen, my dear boy. By God you entered my heart before I even laid eyes upon you. Princess Shayma has told me all about you, and I don't think she loves anyone else. I swear to you I'd do the impossible to help get her out of the king's palace, but until that time comes, I insist that you stay here in our home with us. Don't set foot outside, there are many spies in this city. And any mistake on your part will come with a heavy price for you and me both!"

But I must tell you—come one come all, hear ye hear ye, God guides us and guides you to see—this old woman had been working in the royal palace ever since she was a child, that is, ever since the king I've told you about was just a small boy. When she got older, she was appointed head servant. And because the king trusted her so much, he had entrusted her with taking care of Princess Shayma and attending to her, and he advised her to use all the means at her disposal, including tricks and expertise and guile, to help him get what he was after, but the old woman softened toward Princess Shayma's predicament and started secretly sympathizing with her. When Alaa al-Din came to her asking for aid and assistance, she came up with a foolproof plan to free Princess Shayma from the royal palace.

The next morning, the old woman went to the royal palace as usual. During the afternoon siesta, as all movement quieted down and the king went to nap, she was left all alone with Princess Shayma, at which point she told her about Alaa al-Din, saying, "Tomorrow night you're getting out of this palace!"

"But how?"

"It's all very simple. You'll bind my legs and feet and you'll gag my mouth. Then you'll sneak out of the palace disguised in servant's clothes. You'll meet my husband at the main gate and he'll deliver you to the port, where Alaa al-Din will be waiting for you."

The plan was a success, and Alaa al-Din and Princess Shayma traveled on a merchants' ship heading east. At first, the sea was calm, and the weather was mild. But on the third day, a raging storm fell upon them, and the waves grew to the size of mountains, and the merchants began to pray, beseeching God to deliver them, but the surging waves continued crashing down upon them, and the winds continued violently blowing, and the thunder boomed. In the end, the ship was destroyed and the sea swallowed up everyone on board . . . everyone, that is, except for Alaa al-Din and Princess Shayma. The two of them clung to a board from the destroyed ship, and because they were both good swimmers, the waves carried them to a small island that was shaped like a large boulder. After the storm died down, Alaa al-Din and Princess Shayma washed ashore on that island, which they found to be deserted, and there was nothing on it indicating that human feet had ever stepped upon it before.

Weeks passed, and despair seeped into their souls. Until one morning, they saw a strangely shaped, gigantic bird approach the island and land on one spot. One hour later, it shook out its wings and flew off toward the east. On the second and the third and the fourth day, it was the same thing: the bird alighted on the highest point of the small island, and then flew off toward the east. On the fifth day, Alaa al-Din said to Princess Shayma, "This incredible bird might just be our salvation!"

"But how?"

"We'll grab on to its feet and it might take us back to dry land!"

"Great idea!" said Princess Shayma.

On the sixth day, Alaa al-Din and Princess Shayma approached the peculiar bird, and it didn't recoil from them so they grabbed hold of its feet. After a little while, it flew off toward the east as usual. They were afraid at first, and they felt more than once that the bird could simply drop them into the sea. But they hung on until they spotted dry land, which announced their good fortune. The bird slowly started to descend and landed on a barren hill.

Alaa al-Din looked around him and everything he saw was familiar. Suddenly, he lay down in Princess Shayma's lap and shouted, "We're at the edge of my father's oases, my dear!"

And so it is—come one come all, hear ye hear ye, God guides us and guides you to see—that the fairy tale of Alaa al-Din in the Land of Terrors has come to an end. It will now return to its assigned place in the infinite forest of fairy tales.

May God sustain those who are living!

And have mercy upon those who are dead!

GLOSSARY

Abu al-Qasim al-Shabi (1909–34): a Tunisian poet, best known for penning part of the Tunisian national anthem, and for his anticolonial nationalist activism, which is exemplified in his poem, "To the Tyrants of the World," from which this line is excerpted. Al-Shabi re-entered public culture amid the 2011 uprisings that swept across the Arab world, as many participants circulated this poem in particular.

arbaeen: forty; in Islamic tradition, the fortieth day after the death of a loved one, which is ceremonially commemorated.

Azim Zara: a popular children's game in Tunisia

Azrael: the angel of death in Islamic theology

Farhat Hached (1914–52): a Tunisian nationalist and labor activist, and an associate of other nationalist figures such as Habib Bourguiba. He was assassinated by the *Main Rouge (Red Hand)*, a pro-French terrorist organization in Tunisia.

fatira: a kind of pastry made out of dough, usually stuffed with cheese, vegetables, or meat

Harun al-Rashid: the fifth caliph of the Abbasid empire (r. 786–809), known for promoting scientific, cultural, and religious endeavors; also often identified as the founder of the so-called *bayt al-hikma* ('House of Wisdom') in Baghdad, the Abbasid capital.

Hedi Habbouba: a popular Tunisian Mezoued singer

al-Jazya al-Hilaliya: one of the key figures in the orally transmitted Arabian folk epic Taghribat Bani Hilal, which recounts the tribe of Banu

141

Hilal's journey from Arabia to Tunisia. In North Africa the epic is often referred to as *sirat al-Jazya* (The story of al-Jazya). Al-Jazya al-Hilaliya is described as a paragon of perfection—wise, pragmatic, and beautiful—whose beauty was said to drive men mad. She survives every trial and tribulation and never actually dies in the epic.

Karagöz shadow puppets: *blackeye* in Turkish

malouf: the Arab music of Muslim Andalusia, which spread throughout North Africa, including Tunisia, from the end of the fifteenth century.

Mezoued: a genre of Tunisian popular music, generally associated with the countryside and the working classes, which is often played at weddings and parties. Similar to raï.

Ouled Ayyar: a Berber tribe in Tunisia

Salah el Farzit: a popular Tunisian Mezoued singer

shashiya cap: the deep-red fez worn across the Arab Mediterranean, typically with a gold tassle

Si: an abbreviation for Sidi, which is an honorific meaning 'sir' or 'lord'

Sidi Abd al-Qadir al-Gilani (d. 1166): Born in the Iranian province of Gilan, he studied Hanbali law in Baghdad and later taught there, where he died and was buried; the namesake of the Qadiriya Sufi brotherhood, which enjoys a wide following across the Arab world, Central Asia, and extending into parts of Africa and Europe.

Sidi Abu al-Hasan al-Shadhili (d. 1258): Born in Morocco, al-Shadhili made a spiritual pilgrimage across North Africa, and was eventually buried in Egypt; the namesake of the Shadhiliya Sufi brotherhood, which enjoys a wide following across North Africa, Egypt, and beyond.

Sidi Abdel Salam bin Bashish: spiritual leader (sayid) of Sidi Abu al-Hasan al-Shadhili (see above).

umma: nation, but here a reference to the global community of Muslims

Modern Arabic Literature
from the American University in Cairo Press

Bahaa Abdelmegid *Saint Theresa* and *Sleeping with Strangers*
Ibrahim Abdel Meguid *Birds of Amber* • *Distant Train*
No One Sleeps in Alexandria • *The Other Place*
Yahya Taher Abdullah *The Collar and the Bracelet* • *The Mountain of Green Tea*
Leila Abouzeid *The Last Chapter*
Hamdi Abu Golayyel *A Dog with No Tail* • *Thieves in Retirement*
Yusuf Abu Rayya *Wedding Night*
Ahmed Alaidy *Being Abbas el Abd*
Idris Ali *Dongola* • *Poor*
Rasha al Ameer *Judgment Day*
Radwa Ashour *Granada* • *Specters*
Ibrahim Aslan *The Heron* • *Nile Sparrows*
Alaa Al Aswany *Chicago* • *Friendly Fire* • *The Yacoubian Building*
Fadi Azzam *Sarmada*
Fadhil al-Azzawi *Cell Block Five* • *The Last of the Angels* • *The Traveler and the Innkeeper*
Ali Bader *Papa Sartre*
Liana Badr *The Eye of the Mirror*
Hala El Badry *A Certain Woman* • *Muntaha*
Salwa Bakr *The Golden Chariot* • *The Man from Bashmour* • *The Wiles of Men*
Halim Barakat *The Crane*
Hoda Barakat *Disciples of Passion* • *The Tiller of Waters*
Mourid Barghouti *I Saw Ramallah* • *I Was Born There, I Was Born Here*
Mohamed Berrada *Like a Summer Never to Be Repeated*
Mohamed El-Bisatie *Clamor of the Lake* • *Drumbeat* • *Hunger* • *Over the Bridge*
Mahmoud Darwish *The Butterfly's Burden*
Tarek Eltayeb *Cities without Palms* • *The Palm House*
Mansoura Ez Eldin *Maryam's Maze*
Ibrahim Farghali *The Smiles of the Saints*
Hamdy el-Gazzar *Black Magic*
Randa Ghazy *Dreaming of Palestine*
Gamal al-Ghitani *Pyramid Texts* • *The Zafarani Files* • *Zayni Barakat*
Tawfiq al-Hakim *The Essential Tawfiq al-Hakim*
Yahya Hakki *The Lamp of Umm Hashim*
Abdelilah Hamdouchi *The Final Bet*
Bensalem Himmich *The Polymath* • *The Theocrat*
Taha Hussein *The Days*
Sonallah Ibrahim *Cairo: From Edge to Edge* • *The Committee* • *Zaat*
Yusuf Idris *City of Love and Ashes* • *The Essential Yusuf Idris*
Denys Johnson-Davies *The AUC Press Book of Modern Arabic Literature* • *Homecoming*
In a Fertile Desert • *Under the Naked Sky*
Said al-Kafrawi *The Hill of Gypsies*
Mai Khaled *The Magic of Turquoise*
Sahar Khalifeh *The End of Spring*
The Image, the Icon and the Covenant • *The Inheritance*
Edwar al-Kharrat *Rama and the Dragon* • *Stones of Bobello*